"Grace? Is that you?"

April's voice was frantic. "Grace, are you okay? Where are you?"

The line went dead.

"Oh my God," she said, looking over at Sean. "Do you think...? That couldn't have been her, right? But if it was her... She's alive."

"Who was on the caller ID?" he asked.

"There wasn't a name. It was just a location. It says the number was out of Gillette, Wyoming."

"Call the number back."

She called the number back, but her call went straight to voicemail.

"Damn it!" she yelled, slamming her hand against the dashboard.

"It's okay. Don't get too upset. Maybe it wasn't even her."

She glared at him. "It was her. I know it was Grace. You *know* it was her, too."

He had to hope it wasn't. But the odds of it being anyone else besides Grace were astronomical.

"Sean, she's in trouble. She needs help. She needs us." She looked down at her phone, calling the number again, but it went to voicemail. "There has to be something we can do."

MOUNTAIN ABDUCTION

DANICA WINTERS

INTRIGUE

To Phyllis,
Mama duck's got you

**Harlequin®
INTRIGUE™**

ISBN-13: 978-1-335-59172-2

Mountain Abduction

Copyright © 2024 by Danica Winters

Recycling programs for this product may not exist in your area.

Harlequin Enterprises ULC
22 Adelaide St. West, 41st Floor
Toronto, Ontario M5H 4E3, Canada
www.Harlequin.com

Printed in Lithuania

MIX
Paper | Supporting responsible forestry
FSC® C021394

Danica Winters is a multiple-award-winning, bestselling author who writes books that grip readers with their ability to drive emotion through suspense and occasionally a touch of magic. When she's not working, she can be found in the wilds of Montana, testing her patience while she tries to hone her skills at various crafts—quilting, pottery and painting are not her areas of expertise. She believes the cup is neither half full nor half empty, but it had better be filled with wine. Visit her website at danicawinters.net.

Books by Danica Winters

Harlequin Intrigue

Big Sky Search and Rescue

> *Helicopter Rescue*
> *Swiftwater Enemies*
> *Mountain Abduction*

STEALTH: Shadow Team

> *A Loaded Question*
> *Rescue Mission: Secret Child*
> *A Judge's Secrets*
> *K-9 Recovery*
> *Lone Wolf Bounty Hunter*
> *Montana Wilderness Pursuit*

Stealth

> *Hidden Truth*
> *In His Sights*
> *Her Assassin For Hire*
> *Protective Operation*

Visit the Author Profile page at Harlequin.com.

CAST OF CHARACTERS

April Twofeather—A counselor at Sulphur Springs, an at-risk youth camp, and a woman who's been broken by her past. When the secrets of her former life are revealed, she finds out her future may hold some scary truths.

Sean McCormack—A firefighter and volunteer member of Search and Rescue in Big Sky, Montana. When the chips are down, there is no one better to have at your side.

Grace Bunchen—An at-risk teen who has been constantly torn down by life.

Detective Ty Terrell—The lead detective in Big Sky, and a man who is willing to take a look at situations from all perspectives.

Andrew Blakely—Grace's boyfriend and a fellow camper at Sulphur Springs. He's a kid who is willing to do anything for his first love.

Damon McArthur—April's ex and a man who is desperate to get back into her good graces.

Chapter One

April's lungs ached and her calves where hot and numb from climbing. Her glutes were burning from the near vertical assent of the last push to the rocky and jagged peak in the heart of Montana. Long ago, she and her group of teenage campers had conquered the zigzag trail that had started just outside Big Sky and led halfway up the mountain— the point where most hikers stopped and turned around.

She tried to control her breathing, not daring to seem wanting for air in front of the bloodthirsty teens, the pubescent sharks who waited to feast on any perceived weakness. One of the girls in her group, Grace, had been kicked out of three high schools for possession of weapons, and while April didn't believe the girl would pull a knife on her up here in the woods, she held no doubts that Grace would be the first to slash at her with her condemning words. The girl was brutal.

A few hundred yards downhill, Grace was breathing hard. Her mouth open as she pushed to follow April's path through the loose, rocky scree mountainside. Her green hair was pulled tight against her head, and she was so sweaty that it looked as though she had just stepped out of the shower. There were beads of sweat dripping from her hairline, leaving behind a green tint on her skin thanks to her cheap dye.

When April had been younger, she and her delinquent friends had used Kool-Aid to color their hair, and the results were much the same. It was a strange comfort to see that some things hadn't changed in the sixteen years since she left high school—*left* might have been a slight exaggeration, as she'd been more or less kicked out after she'd found out she was pregnant.

Her hand drifted down to her abdomen as she thought about the baby that had once been hers. If she could guide other kids through the woods, maybe she, in some simple way, could help them navigate their lives and lead them to realize that no matter what life confronted them with, they had the power to break through and conquer the nearly vertical assents.

"Push past the pain, Grace," she called, trying not to sound placating or cloying in her attempt to encourage the girl.

This was Grace's battle, and only she could find the inner strength to keep going, but April could be there to give her support and celebrate with her for the well-earned and empowering victory that came with conquering the mountain. The mountain was a metaphor for so many things in her life, so many choices, so many mistakes and opportunities that she had failed to grasp.

As much as April wanted to think that she wouldn't continue to fail in her life—that instead this one personal victory would be enough to change her forever and free her of being the imperfect human she'd become—she held no false hopes. There would forever be more mountains to climb. Though she would like to think she could conquer them all, there would be times she failed. It was only when she stopped trying to press her way to the top—when she gave up and let the challenges beat her—that she would truly lose, and she would be losing a part of herself.

Perhaps that was the lesson she wanted Grace and the three other kids who followed behind her on the mountain to realize. Each kid had their own demons and hardships to overcome, but she'd love to think she could give them the tools and fortitude to keep pressing.

Grace had stopped and was looking up at her from down the mountain. "This had better be worth it," the girl growled between breaths. "This is the stupidest thing you've had us do, yet."

"If you wanted something easy, you could have signed up for basket weaving."

"I should have," Grace said, trying to catch her breath. "At least then I wouldn't have had to stare at your ass in my face for the last three miles."

She wanted to be mad at the girl for her rudeness, but something about her fire made April check her laugh. Grace was nothing if not authentic and that had to be appreciated to some degree.

"You know, they make creams for cellulite, now," Grace snarled. "If you're going to wear tight pants, you should probably shell out the money."

Strike that, she thought, *the girl is an authentic ass.*

Any approbation she had been feeling with the girl blew away on the high-mountain wind. To argue with her would be an admission that Grace had hurt her feelings, but to let the comment go without rebuttal was to give Grace the win in letting her rudeness go without consequence. Yet, on this mountain, there were better things than words to use in this clash.

She considered making the girl pick up one of the rocks at her feet and put it in her backpack to carry as some symbolic weight about the pain that could be left by words. This girl was the kind who would never respond to physical punishments, but she also wasn't the kind who would follow the rules.

Maybe Grace was April's real battle, not the hike.

She sidestepped around the loose rock near the top, carefully planting her feet as she moved down the steep hill and reached out for Grace. "Here, take my hand."

The girl sneered at her hand and pushed it away. "I don't need help."

"I know you don't want it, but learning when to accept help when it is provided is a strength in itself." She motioned for her to take her hand.

The other three kids finally came around the corner and into view, looking more tired than even she felt. One of the boys, Andrew, in the back was ruddy faced and he had taken off his jacket and had tied it around his waist.

"I've got this," Grace said quietly, as though she did not want the others to hear.

Grace looked over her shoulder at the group and, instead of taking her hand, she moved farther away and toward an area that was even steeper than where April had chosen to make their final ascent.

With every step Grace took, the rocky crumbling hillside shifted and gave way, the incline too steep to allow for any additional pressure. Grace's face pinched into a tight, resolved scowl as she grabbed at the rocks and moved her body lower toward the ground to move her weight to her advantage.

She gained a few feet before the rocks she had been standing on shifted and gave way, creating a clacking of granite on granite as the cobbles smacked against boulders and scattered downward.

Yesterday, it had rained on the mountain, leaving the ground saturated to the point where a major slide was very possible, but something like that was rare. Though, a decade or so ago, a family had been killed in a situation much like this on this mountain. She didn't want to be a headline or a tragedy others spoke about around campfires and wine circles as some cautionary tale.

"Grace, get over here," she said, trying to sound calm as she watched a rock plummet and explode as it hit a boulder.

The girl didn't look at her. "I said I've got this," she growled through her teeth.

April moved closer, careful to stay where it was less steep. She reached down to her side where she had a rope tied to her in case of emergencies. "Listen," she ordered, trying to sound calm but also clear that she meant business, "you need to move toward me, slowly."

More rocks slipped downhill from Grace's feet. The entire hillside where she stood was unstable. If they didn't move quickly, the girl would undoubtedly find herself at the center of a full, earth-shattering rockslide.

Her mind moved to the phone call she would have to make to Grace's foster mother explaining that her daughter had been killed on April's watch. She couldn't make that phone call, not now and not ever.

"I said—" Grace started.

"I don't care what you think you *can* do. I'm telling you,

right now, if you don't come toward me and get out of the center of that unstable rock, you will be the next thing tumbling down that hill."

Grace shot her a look like she was trying to decide which was more important—her pride or her welfare.

The girl started to move toward April.

There were the sounds of clattering stones behind April, and she turned to see the other three kids moving toward her. "Stay back!" she ordered, louder and sounding more frightened than she had intended.

The kids behind her stopped moving, but there was the same sound of clattering rocks below them that had come with Grace's attempt to climb.

She turned to face the small group. "I want you to start picking your way back to where you came from."

"But, Ms. Twofeather," Andrew argued, motioning toward the top of the mountain, clearly unaware of the situation they seemed to be finding themselves in—one she wasn't about to explain. "I didn't come this far to give up now."

"Just follow my orders," she countered, her heart racing as she watched another rock give way, which caused a little rockslide below her. "Go back. *Now.*"

Andrew frowned, but then motioned for the group to follow him back. She watched as they moved, but she was careful to stay still in an attempt to mollify the groaning and shifting mountain.

There were old tales of miners who were looking for rich deposits of Montana gold and silver who heard the mountain call to them before tragedies would strike. Often, the miners would hear moans and thumping that they called "Tommyknockers," and they had become so well-known that miners would rush to evacuate their shafts.

She turned back to Grace as she attempted to get her heart rate under control.

April wanted to move to the girl, to anchor her with the rope so that they would have their combined strengths in case something happened, but adding more pressure to the crumbling slope was foolish. "Come my way, Grace," she said, speaking softly like to a newborn foal.

There was a moan, but the sound didn't come from Grace or any human. Her body clenched at the ghostly sound. The mountain was warning.

"Hurry!" April said, motioning toward the girl. "We have to get out of here. The whole hillside is going to give way."

Grace looked down the mountain. Her hands searched for her next grip as the rock beneath her started to slip.

"Come!" April stood her ground though she wanted to lunge toward Grace and save her.

Grace sprang from the rock and scrambled toward her as the rocks beneath her started to move like sand, sinking and pulsing with each step and pull.

As Grace got near, April grabbed for her, but as she did, the mountain beneath her crumbled.

Neither was safe.

There was no one coming to their rescue, no one who *could* rescue them. Her feet slipped as she moved to cover Grace with her body.

"Hold on to me. Don't let go," she ordered, pulling Grace into her embrace as the world around them fell to pieces.

Grace cried out with fear. It felt as though they were atop a concrete wave. The world spun. Pain rattled through April's body as she flipped and turned, crashing against the ground. A rock hit her hard in the ribs, making a cracking sound.

The dust created by the granite stones hitting one another, filled with shimmering mica, coated her mouth and skin like wayward glitter.

Falling, Grace's arms tightened around her, her nails digging into her flesh.

They weren't going to make it out of this alive.

The mountain they had come to conquer was now hellbent to destroy.

Chapter Two

Sean McCormack was attempting to sleep. These days, every moment seemed to be filled with either the needs of his job as a firefighter or those of his group at Big Sky Search and Rescue. They'd had three callouts this week, all lost hikers. In the last seven days, Sean had hiked more than seventy miles.

He was exhausted.

Yet, as he thought about the last call—an elderly couple who'd gotten turned around on a trail and found themselves five miles farther into the backcountry than they had intended—he found it nearly impossible to sleep. He pinched his eyes closed, trying.

On his last shift at the firehouse, he'd been up for so many hours that he wasn't sure he hadn't seen an Oompa Loompa skipping around in their kitchen—then again, that could have been his buddy Steve who loved acting a fool when they had downtime. The lucky bastard.

Sometimes it felt like he still lived in a frat house, albeit this time there were both men and women. Everything was always moving no matter the time, things were in a constant state of needing repair, there were unidentifiable smells and everyone was always hungry. The biggest difference was the lack of kegs. Many of the younger guys made up for this on their off time, though, and one even prided himself on brewing his own craft IPAs like he was Hank Schrader from *Breaking Bad*—complete with a few bottles blowing up in his garage and pissing his wife off in the process.

Yep, I'm never going to sleep.

His phone buzzed on the bedside table. He sat up and rubbed his face. The bed creaked under his weight, a victim of too many sleepless nights.

He clicked on the notification on his phone. There was a missing woman and girl, known victims of a rockslide on the back side of Lone Mountain, just outside the ski resort's boundaries. The peak was more than eleven thousand feet above sea level, and it was a hell of a backbreaker. Most people didn't make it to the top, as the easiest route up was nearly vertical and so high that the peak was well above the tree line.

He let the SAR group know that he was available and would take the callout.

They'd meet at the trailhead where they'd be briefed about the situation, and each given their assignments.

Do we have an ID on the vics? he texted Cindy Des-Champs, the head of SAR.

She was a good chick and super great as their leader. She took no crap and was a positive influence on the team. She could bring people together and diffuse problems like no one else he'd ever met.

There was a pause and then the distinctive dots as she started to type her response.

Her texted popped up: Looks like it was a woman and a girl from the Sulfur Springs At-Risk Youth Group. Girl is sixteen, Grace Bunchen. The counselor is April Twofeather.

His stomach sank. April Twofeather, seriously? He'd gone to high school with April. Then again, who didn't he go to high school with within his age bracket? In this small town, everyone knew everyone and *everything*. Though he and April had shared a few classes, he hadn't been on good terms with her, especially when everyone in the school had found out she had gotten pregnant.

Not long after, she had disappeared from the school. Rumor had it that she was too embarrassed to show her face. She'd been dating Cameron Blakely. The thought of the guy and his tragic death made Sean's stomach clench. The day Cameron had died had been one of the worst days of Sean's life.

Some people swore the baby wasn't Cameron's, but Sean had known better. After Cameron died, April had been rubbing elbows with a lot of college-aged guys who came over to Big Sky to ski for a week—but who hadn't? From November to March, there was a constant flow of ski bums from surrounding areas and abroad. Locals had their pick. There was always a line of fresh gossip.

Then again, if gossip was to be believed, Sean had also bedded more than his fair share of ski bunnies and, according to one juicy story he'd heard about himself, he'd even shared a bed with two at the same time. If only his life was that interesting. Though, if he had a chance in real life, he wasn't sure he'd take it—that sounded like something he could fail at, and failure in that department wasn't an option. He'd take one good woman over many any day.

His phone buzzed again, pulling him from his thoughts of the past.

The SAR team would meet on Lone Mountain. From his house, it wasn't too far a drive, but the dirt roads leading to there were notoriously rutted and, after yesterday's rain, would be like driving in Silly Putty.

He grabbed his go bag and hit the road, listening to the radio chatter between the SAR team members as he headed in their direction. It sounded like Cindy and her boyfriend were already at the trailhead and there would be four two-member teams to look for the missing females.

He had been right about the Silly Putty, and as he hit the logging road leading to their access point, he had to put his vehicle in four-wheel drive to keep from sliding around. April was probably as used to these kinds of roads as he was if she had felt comfortable in taking on the behemoth of a mountain.

With this level of ground saturation, it was no wonder that they had found themselves at the epicenter of a rockslide. On this mountain, rockslides weren't a normal occurrence, but not unheard of—they were like lightning.

He wanted to mentally condemn April for choosing this hike in these kinds of conditions, but he would be hard-pressed to say that he would have done anything different. Yet, it was that very "it won't happen to me" mentality that often kept him and his teammates both at SAR and the fire department busy.

Cindy was waiting beside her pickup when he arrived. She was dressed in layers and was going through her hiking backpack. She looked up and gave him a smile and a wave as he slogged up to the little parking area at the bottom of the trail.

Mud caked the outside of his pickup, and as he got out and slammed the door a chunk dropped from behind his tire. "How's it going, Cindy?"

She gave him a little nod. "So far, our two teams are a go.

The two other teams are going to start at the next trailhead over. I want us to work the possible edges of the rockslide without having to cross over any potentially questionable conditions."

She was right. The last thing they needed to do was to cause another slide.

"Has anyone seen or heard from the missing females? Any cell phone pings?" he asked.

Chad, Cindy's boyfriend, stood up on the other side of the pickup. "We had Detective Leo West run a pinpoint on April's phone. We have a general idea of where her phone was last picked up by the towers, but as you know it isn't exact. Plus, given the conditions, the phone may not be with her if she had been carrying it in a backpack—or it could be buried."

Thank you, Captain Obvious. As much as he liked Cindy, he wasn't as much of a fan of Chad.

The guy had pushed his way onto their team, and though he definitely had the chops to be a member, it gnawed at Sean that Chad was an automatic walk-on when everyone else had to go through a heavy vetting process. There were few things more irritating than an out-of-stater expecting to get what they wanted without so much as a written test, and it going in their favor.

He sighed, reminding himself not to be too salty. A good addition to the team was a good addition, regardless of the methods in which they had taken to get there.

Besides, sometimes the best teams were made up of people who weren't necessarily best friends. It created an environment where everyone still wanted to prove their value-add and be at their best physical levels. Since Chad

had joined his team, Sean had made sure to add twenty-reps when he lifted.

"How many other kids were with the females?" Sean asked.

Cindy stood up after closing her bag. "There were five in total. The other three, two boys and a girl, are at the local hospital getting checked for any injuries. They said they had rushed out after the rockslide, but they were all hit with falling debris from the slide. One of the boys had a pretty good shiner." She touched the area under her left eye.

"I hope they're all okay," he said, as another truck rolled up with Steve, who was assigned to his team today.

It didn't take them long to hit the mountainside, but the climb was brutal. He could almost imagine the whining and moaning the high school kids must have been dishing out on their nearly vertical assent. He was huffing by the time they hit their fifth switchback on the trail and the altitude started to take its toll.

Cindy paused for a minute on a larger area in the switchback where they could all catch up and hear one another. Steve was still smiling, which irked him. This guy didn't appear to be in any better shape than him. Thankfully, Chad was pulling up the rear and his face was red, he was winded and beads of sweat were pouring down from his temples.

"We are going to split up here," Cindy said, motioning toward the continuing switchbacks. "I want you and Steve to work the rockslide from here, up. According to the kids, this is where the slide kind of played out."

He nodded, trying not to speak to hide the fact that he was struggling to catch his breath and get his heart rate under control.

"Let's touch base every hour or so," Cindy continued. "We will hike up another couple hundred yards and work the edge so we don't kick things loose, but we can cover more area. I want you to work the left half of the main slide. The other teams will be doing the same on the other side."

"Got it," he clipped.

"Good luck, guys," Cindy said, turning toward the trail but giving them one look back over her shoulder. "And make sure you watch for any falling rocks. As we all know, this is an unstable environment. While we need to work fast, we also need to make sure we work safely."

"Let's find these ladies alive," Steve added, like it was their call to arms.

Steve was one hell of a guy and, not for the first time, Sean was glad to have him on his side.

He and Steve carefully picked a lateral line on the mountain and steadily moved to the north. Coming around the top of the ridge, the slide came into view. It was massive. Tons upon tons of loose rock had poured down the mountain and even though it had happened more than four hours ago, there was still a strange taste of dust in the air.

There was no way these women were still alive.

Given the conditions, he didn't want to call out to April and Grace if it were to cause more of the mountain to break loose. But before they found themselves victims of the slide, this was the time. They wouldn't get another opportunity.

Steve looked over at him as he came to a stop. "What's up?"

"You think we should give a shout?"

"If these two are alive, I want them to know we're looking for them. Or if they're sitting on the edge of this slide or injured somewhere… Well, *you know*. But what if you trigger another slide?" he countered.

Sean pinched his lips. "We have to hope that I won't, but I know for a fact that we are the first ones on scene. We need to make a choice."

Steve sucked in a long breath and scanned the rockslide like they were looking at a field of grave markers. "Do it."

"April! Grace!" He held for a second. "April Twofeather, this is Sean McCormack with Big Sky Search and Rescue! Call out if you can!"

He waited for the telltale sound of falling rocks but was instead met with the feeble sounds of a woman's cry. She sounded like a hurt animal, and the sound tore at his soul.

"April?"

She gave a warbled call. The sound came from above them on the hill, and he rushed toward it with Steve close on his heels.

Picking through the edge of the fall, weaving between boulders, he came over a small knob. Sitting on a rock, bloodied and battered, was April Twofeather.

"April," he said, relief filling his voice, "we're gonna get you out of here."

She looked up at him, her right eye was nearly swollen shut and black and purple. Her arm was hanging at a weird angle and blood streaked down the legs of her pants. Tears poured down her cheeks. "I'm…I'm sorry," she said between ragged breaths, which made him question whether she was suffering from some broken ribs as well.

"You have nothing to be sorry for." He moved to her and dropped to his knees. He wanted to ask her if she knew where the girl was, but from the state she was in, he doubted she'd be able to answer. He gently put his hand on her leg as he looked up at her. "Don't worry. I've got you. I'll get the helo in here and get you airlifted out."

"What… Where…" she said, wheezing.

"Don't worry, we will. You can trust me." He smiled, trying to bring her comfort. "Steve, you wanna call in Casper and have the air crew roll in? Make sure they steer clear of any unstable areas."

Steve nodded. "Already on it," he said, tapping on his phone. "Cindy said they spotted Grace above. They aren't to her yet, but she is alive."

April started to sob.

Sean rubbed her shoulder gently, and she softened under his touch. "We've got you guys…you're safe."

And, thankfully, still alive.

Chapter Three

There was a man. He'd appeared in a halo of dust in the evening sun. She had to squint to focus, but even squinting it was like she was looking through water. He couldn't be real. Not with those blue eyes. They were the same color as the headwaters when they came out of the mountains. Maybe she had died, and this was some kind of afterlife that pooled her perfect location and her ideal man.

She glanced around, looking for more familiar faces, but he was the only person she could see. This had to be real, this moment. Yet, what was he doing here?

A warm drip moved down from her temple. Reaching up, she touched the liquid and brought it down. Her fingertips were covered in blood. *Her blood.*

"April..." the familiar man said, but his voice was muddled and heavy, like it was coming from an antique gramophone. "You're going to be okay."

She tried to recall how she had gotten here. She was sitting on a rock.

Rockslide.

The world collapsing around her.

Pain. So much pain.

"Grace! Where's Grace?" she cried. She tried to stand up, but her body was wracked with pain...it hurt *everywhere*.

Her head spun, making her close her eyes, and she plopped down.

"Grace is up the hill. She didn't fall as far as you." The man was touching her shoulder. His fingers were cool against her feverish skin. "She said you covered her with your body."

She remembered moving toward Grace and pulling her into her. Then the darkness.

Kids? What...about the others? she tried to ask, but there was a sharp pain in her chest as she tried to breathe.

A wave of nausea washed over her as the stabbing from her ribs broke through the adrenaline-induced anesthesia.

"Sick... I'm going to be sick," she said, her deep breaths only compounding the agony.

The man said something, but he sounded like he was far away and moving farther. He couldn't leave her. She needed him. She needed help.

He said something about getting her on a board and moving her to a safe place for the helicopter. As she looked up at him, the world started to disappear around his halo like some monster was trying to devour him and her world. The darkness moved fast, and the beast swallowed them whole.

THE NEXT MORNING Sean sat in the corner of April's room in the ER after he'd made sure Grace was squared away in the pediatric ward. Grace had a sprained wrist and was doing well, but they wanted to keep her overnight for observation. It was amazing how much better she had fared than April.

The doctors had given April a heavy dose of pain meds to keep her comfortable. From what they had told him, they were waiting to get her into CT to get a scan—it was possible, given her fall, that she could be suffering from some kind of head or neck injury.

The Bozeman hospital had been the closest, and they were a good Level III trauma center, but they were limited thanks to a large car accident on I-90 and patients had stacked up. Maybe he'd made a mistake in having Casper and his team fly her here instead of a larger hospital like one in Seattle or Salt Lake City.

He hoped beyond all hope that she would only be dealing with what they had already found—so far, a concussion, a dark bruise on her face, cracked ribs and her right arm had been broken in several places.

The nurse in charge of her care walked in with a new bag of IV fluids. "How's our girl doing?" she asked, like it was just any other day in the ER, and he hadn't pulled this woman off the mountain after a catastrophic slide yesterday.

"She hasn't moved," he said, trying not to laugh at the inanity of his statement. Of course she hadn't budged, but he wasn't really sure what else the nurse could have expected him to say. "Did you manage to get in touch with one of her emergency contacts?"

The nurse shook her head as she hung up the bag and set about her work with the lines. "I called the man she had on file. It was her father. Unfortunately, it sounds like he has passed. I asked the woman who answered if there was anyone there who was related to April or knew her, but it sounded like she was on her own. I've given the search over to social work to see if they can make more headway. It always bothers me when patients are here alone—many don't recover, or their recovery is greatly slowed when they don't have support."

Just like him, April was alone in the world. It made an odd, hollow sensation build within his chest.

The nurse gave him a grateful smile. "You know, she is lucky to have you."

If she had been lucky, I would have never been called to her rescue, he thought as he rubbed at the back of his neck. *My being here only proves how unlucky she really is.*

"I don't know about that," he said, brushing off the nurse's well-intended but naive compliment.

He glanced over at April; her blond hair was dirty and matted with blood and dust, and her eye had gotten impossibly darker. He had never noticed how pretty she was when they had been growing up, but then again he couldn't say that he had ever really looked at her before.

It felt strange looking at her like this and thinking her beautiful. Or maybe it wasn't. It was a helluva thing to be at a person's worst and still be good-looking. When she made it through this, which she *had to*, he would have liked to see how she presented herself to the world.

"We are going to be taking her down for her CT in five minutes," the nurse said. "You are welcome to wait here until she gets back."

He looked down at his clothes. He was covered in blood—*her blood*.

"I'm going to run to Peds and check on Grace, then I'll go home and clean up. I'll come back to check on her in a few hours," he said, but as he did there was a pull inside of him. It could have been partly what the nurse said about dismal recovery rates when abandoned, but he didn't want to leave April's bedside.

He tried to tell himself that his being there didn't matter—and that the nurse was just trying to get him to stay. April didn't even know he was here, and if by some reason she did know, she wouldn't recognize him. When someone went through an event like hers, oftentimes they forgot the immediate aftermath—it was as if the brain protected itself from the trauma of major incidents by wiping the slate clean…well, mostly.

He knew from personal experience how some forgotten horrors came back—normally in the middle of the night. He always feared when life was going too well, as it seemed to be in those moments of relative peace and calm, that the horrors would come to life.

The memories were part of the reason he'd gone into firefighting—through his work, he had learned to control his fear and keep the nightmares mostly at bay.

"Sean?" the nurse asked, pulling him back to reality and away from the blood that was splattered over the legs of his pants from when he'd helped get April on the board and into the helo.

"Yeah, sorry. What?" he asked.

The nurse frowned. "You probably need to get some sleep." She started to adjust April's bed as she readied it to wheel down to Imaging.

"Yeah," he said, his exhaustion hitting him as he stood up from the pink vinyl chair he'd been sitting in. He hated those damned chairs.

"Make sure you drive home safely… Better yet, you should get a ride." The nurse clicked down the bed's side rail.

He walked toward the door, trying to cover a yawn. As he reached the door, he turned back to face the nurse and April. He looked over at the dark-haired woman from his past. "If I'm not back in time to talk to the doctor, please give me a call if there are any changes. Okay?"

The woman gave him a sweet smile. "You got it, Sean."

He tipped his head and moved toward the Peds Unit. His hiking boots still had dirt in them, and there was a click on the tile as he walked like there was a pebble stuck in the treads. It was strange how such a little thing could be so annoying.

It was, however, a welcome change of thought from April and all the things he could have done differently and more effectively in her and Grace's rescue. Though they had gotten to them rather quickly, he wondered if he could have shaved off time. Maybe they should have called in the helo before they even arrived on scene.

All through the night, he had questioned every move they'd made—if they'd only arrived a few minutes earlier, maybe it would have made a difference if April was dealing with head trauma. If their lag had led to some sort of brain damage, he wouldn't be able to look himself in the mirror.

No. I have to stop, he told himself for the hundredth time. *We did the best we could. We were fast. Yes, we could have been faster, but we did well.*

He wasn't really paying attention to the world around him as he walked on autopilot thanks to his exhaustive self-flagellation. He turned the corner toward Grace's room. A nurse came hurrying out, rushing toward their station.

He was pulled back to reality.

"What's going on?" he asked but the nurse ignored him, and he rushed toward Grace's room. Her bed was ruffled, but empty. He hurried toward the station, hoping to get the nurse's attention. "Hello? What happened to her? Where's Grace?" he asked, his stomach clenching with panic.

The nurse turned to look at him. "Who are you?"

"Where is she?" he countered, not wanting to play the stupid song and dance. "Is she okay?"

The nurse looked him over, her gaze stopping at the dried blood on his pants. "Grace…" She looked up at him and there was a panic in her eyes. "Grace is *missing*."

Chapter Four

When April woke up, it took her a minute to make sense of her surroundings. Pink vinyl chair. A window that looked out onto a brick wall. Why would anyone put a window against a wall?

It was like some cruel joke—a teasing, speck of sun only to be captured and entrapped.

It had been two days of lying in her hospital bed, and she felt more trapped with each passing minute. If there was a hell, this was it. If it hadn't been for the monotonous beeps of IV pumps and occasional blaring of machines, she was almost sure that she would have been able to hear the *tick, tick, tick* of the clock on the wall, and it would have driven her to madness.

She picked up her phone, checking her emails. Everyone from Sulphur Springs had been surprisingly quiet. The kids from the trip had sent her get-well texts, but no one had texted in the last day and a half. She'd sent out a few messages to the other counselor at the camp, Kimberly, but the only response she'd gotten was: "Don't worry. We've got everything handled."

Maybe they were all trying to let her rest. In the last day and a half, most of her time had been spent sleeping. Her nurses had told her that a man involved in getting her off the mountain had popped in. She was almost relieved he hadn't woken her up. She wasn't sure how she was supposed to adequately thank a person who was responsible for saving her life. A simple "Thank you" would never do, but the next best thing she could come up with was a fist bump and thanks to her bruised hands, even that was out of the question.

It felt like there wasn't a single location on or within her body that didn't hurt. She'd like to hope that every inch of her would start to get less tender and sore, but any time she tried to move she was reminded about all the hidden bruises.

There was a knock on the door. "Yes?" she called.

"I'm here to take you dancing," a man said. His voice was familiar, but she couldn't quite place him. "That is, if you are decent. You dressed?"

She pulled the dusty-rose-colored blanket up around her chin, the waffled texture imprinting on her skin as she held it tightly. "It's hard to say I'm dressed. I saw what all these gowns cover—or *don't*—in the mirror earlier. However, you are welcome to come in."

The man walked in and the sight of him made her jaw drop. "Heya, April." He sent her a smile that made her more aware than ever that she wasn't wearing any underwear. She pulled the blanket tighter against her body as she tried to control her embarrassment at feeling so vulnerable and exposed.

"I didn't think you were real," she said, nearly stumbling over her words like they were two left feet.

He pressed his hands to his chest and felt around his body in a way that made her want to do the same. "Last time I checked I was a real boy."

There is that damned stunning grin, again.

She had to look away so no more color would rise into her cheeks. She stared at the blank brick wall outside like it was the Mona Lisa.

"Wait," the man continued, "you aren't seeing anyone else in the room, are you? Ghosts or something?"

She jerked back to face him, but she was met with that damned grin again. "No. No ghosts." She ran her hand over her hair and decided to fight fire with fire, and she sent him the best and most seductive grin she could muster in her battered state.

"So, no hallucinations that I should be concerned about?" he teased.

Unless he counted the one in which he'd had a halo...

"Only the one where you think you will be taking me dancing," she said, smiling up at him and hating to admit that she was enjoying his charm. "You know, I was thinking if you sprung me from this joint, that we could do something...*bigger*."

He quirked his brow. "Bigger? Than dancing? Impossible."

She gave a little jerk of her head, teen-like. "Oh...heck yes. I was thinking we take to the sky—take a leap of faith and skydive."

He tilted his head back with a laugh. "I like your style," he said between laughs. "However, I'm not one for leaps of faith...or skydiving for that matter."

"That's strange," she said, her smile widening.

"What is?" he asked, leaning against the window frame and crossing his arms over his chest.

"Well, you are asking me to commit to a leap when you wouldn't do the same."

"How's that?" he asked, frowning.

She didn't like when his smile disappeared, the loss made her room seem substantially colder. "Well, you walked into my room here, you make jokes, and yet, I have no idea who you are."

The warmth returned. "Oh, I see…"

"Yes, for all I know you are here to kill me. Some kind of murder-for-hire plot. I mean look at me," she said, finally letting the blanket fall from her hands as she waved over her body, "I've never been more vulnerable. The only real question would be what kind of weapon you'd use to do the job."

"Do you have a lot of people who want you dead?" He sounded genuinely concerned, bringing her back to the reality of her current situation.

"I was joking around," she said, avoiding her fears and trying to keep things from getting too dark. "You still haven't told me your name."

"Yeah, man, sorry. I'm Sean McCormack. I'm the one who found you."

"Oh…" She covered her mouth with her hand, embarrassed that she hadn't recognized the man she had been fearing to see.

He shrugged. "Don't feel bad. You were under stress and then the mind plays tricks on you to help you keep from reliving the trauma of the event." He looked away from her, and she wasn't sure, but she could have almost sworn he'd looked let down. "Actually, the science behind trauma is incredibly interesting." He kept yammering on about psychology, like he was feeling as awkward as she was.

"I'm familiar with a few of those points," she said, trying to win back his favor and possibly his friendship. He had saved her life. "I'm sure you know, but I work with kids—"

"At Sulphur Springs. Yep," he said, finishing her sentence. "You know, though, we actually went to high school together as well."

She tried to recall him from those days, but all she could think about of her time in high school were the tough decisions she had been forced to make and the baby she had given up for adoption when none of the family wanted to step up and help. For the second time in as many minutes, she found herself at a loss and embarrassed by her poor memory.

"Don't worry about it," he offered, clearly sensing her discomfort. "I'm actually kind of glad you don't remember me. Those adolescent years weren't some of my best."

"Mine, either," she said.

His face pinched, and she knew that her reputation from those years had preceded her.

Damn it. She took a breath. *There goes the rest of my chances in making him fall for me.*

He shifted against the window and his feet pointed toward the door. The poor man was right in wanting to run. Before he could, she needed to say her piece.

"Sean, no thank you is enough for what you did for me and the kids I was with. If there's anything I can do to repay you or your unit, please let me know."

His look of discomfort deepened as he seemed to shrink in upon himself. "Actually, there was something I was hoping to talk to you about, something you might be able to help me with."

"Anything." She pressed down the edge of her blanket

and smoothed the fabric like she could brush away all the strange edges of this moment.

"Has anyone talked to you about Grace?"

She looked up at him, and some of the blood receded from her face. "Is she okay? The last thing I heard was that she was doing well. Did something change?" She asked her questions in a single, frenzied breath.

"Unfortunately, she has gone missing." He straightened slightly. "I talked to the local police, and they say they're doing everything they can, but given her age and her checkered past, they don't seem to be doing much to find her."

"But she's missing!" How dare they not go after Grace just because she had made mistakes in her life. Especially considering how horribly life had treated her up to this point—she'd been bouncing between low-level foster homes, given up by parents who she had helped care for while they dealt with the ravages of fentanyl addiction, and in high school...well, the teachers and her peers could sense the girl's weakness. Now even the police were letting her down.

They were making a villain of a victim.

Her blood pressure spiked on the monitor by her bedside.

"That's why I'm here." He moved closer to her and put his arm on her shoulder. "I needed to find out if you knew where she might have gone or who she might have run away with."

"You don't think she was kidnapped?" she countered, upset that Grace was automatically at fault.

He raised a brow like he was questioning whether someone would actually want to spend time with such a difficult teen. "Right now, they don't even know how she made it out of the hospital without being seen."

April sat up straighter. "This place must be covered in cameras. There has to be something to tell us about what happened to Grace."

"She didn't show up on any of their recordings. They started looking this morning, but…" He trailed off as he looked out at the brick wall. "I'm worried about her. I just need to know she's okay. Do you know her foster parents?"

Grace hadn't been overly chatty with April about her family situation, which was true to form about most of the kids she had worked with at the camp. "These kids aren't the type who are born with silver spoons in their mouths. Most of them are wards of the state or struggling through the foster system."

He nodded. "We tried to contact her foster family, but they haven't been answering their phone. My buddy at the sheriff's department said they drove out there, but no one was around."

"Did they talk to other kids who might have been in her foster home? Her friends from the camp?" She moved gingerly to the side of her bed, swinging her legs over the side. The sudden movement made her ribs ache, and she had to pause to catch her breath.

"What are you doing?" he asked. "Can I help you get something?"

"Yeah, you can help me get the hell out of here. There's no way I'm going to sit in Club Med here while Grace is still missing. I can't let the world give up on her, and no matter what happened to her, she needs help."

Chapter Five

Sean didn't agree with her leaving the hospital. April was there for a reason, and though he had teased her about springing her from the joint, it hadn't really been his plan. She needed to heal and get better, or she did no one any good and had the potential to be more of a liability than an asset. Though he had gently tried to explain all of that to her when she had stepped behind the curtain and gotten dressed, it hadn't stopped her from going AMA—or, against medical advice.

They'd slipped out of the room and down the hall without a nurse even taking notice.

"Don't you think we should just wait until you are officially discharged?" he asked.

"I let the nurse know I was leaving. They said they had to wait for the paperwork from the doctor, but I don't care."

He slowed down, looking back at the nurses' station. No one was around, and there were beeps coming from one of the rooms where the staff must be. "Are you sure?"

She nodded and walked ahead. "All they are doing is giving me NSAIDs at this point. I'll be fine. CT came back clean."

As they walked down the stairs and made their way outside and into the parking lot, it had struck him how and why Grace had been able to disappear so easily—the nurses were overworked and understaffed; they could only do so much, and babysitting wasn't on their list of duties. He felt bad that they were the ones who had been questioned at length about Grace's disappearance. No doubt, her nurse had taken a stern talking-to as a minor had gone missing. Hopefully, she hadn't lost her job when so much was out of her hands.

April got into his pickup and stared out the window. Her face was expressionless, but he could tell she was struggling with Grace's disappearance. He didn't want to scare her with all the possibilities, or how little they could really do to help the girl. "How's your arm feeling? Did you get some pain meds this morning or do we need to stop and grab you some?"

April glanced over at him. She lifted her pink-casted arm slightly, as if reminding herself that she had a broken wing. "It's fine. I have a bit of a headache, but that can happen after a concussion."

"You should have stayed—"

She put up her good hand, waving him quiet. "I would have been getting out today anyway. I'm going to be fine. The only thing I'm worried about is finding Grace. Her foster family trusted me with her care. The last thing I could do was sit around and wait for her to be found."

He couldn't argue. He wasn't the kind to sit around and wait, either.

"When was she last seen?" April asked, looking over at him.

"She disappeared almost as soon as she was moved up to the pediatric floor."

"So, two nights ago?" She ran her hand over her face

in exasperation. "She could be just about anywhere by now. Why didn't you tell me before? Why didn't *anyone*?"

"I was out looking for her, coordinating with law enforcement. They did their best, but their hands are tied."

"Wait…" She paused, staring at him. "You're not a cop?"

He shook his head.

"Then what are you doing here?"

"I told you. I want to make sure she is safe."

"Why? She's not your kid," she countered, but as soon as she spoke her hand flew over her mouth in embarrassment. "That didn't come out right. I…I just mean…"

"I know it's not conventional for a firefighter to be out here working the beat for a missing kid, but I'm also part of a search and rescue team, and this is a small town and I feel like I can make a difference. I also knew how much Grace going missing was going to bother you. Last night, when you were pretty heavily medicated, you were saying her name in your sleep."

She opened her mouth like she was going to say something, but then snapped it shut.

"If you don't want me helping to search for Grace, I can bow out, but like you…I just can't stand sitting idly by when there is something I can be doing."

He was tempted to tell her more, but he didn't want to do April any more harm. She already had enough to deal with without him dumping on her.

"SAR is part of this search, still?" she asked, cocking her head to one side.

She was making him want to tell her the truth, but he wasn't ready. Yet, he didn't need to come off like some kind of over-reaching psycho, either. He shook his head.

"No. I'm working this while I'm off. I have the next couple of days before I have my next shift at the fire station."

"Oh," she said, nodding slightly like his being a first responder helped make sense of why he was acting so altruistic. "Is that why you are so ready and willing to go out of your way to find her? You are always a hero?"

He threw his head back with a laugh. "Not hardly. Everyone in Big Sky is keeping an eye out for this girl."

"Okay," she said, shooting him a smile. "But why?" she pressed. "What's in this search for *you*?"

She wasn't letting it go, and it was *killing* him. He pulled out onto the road leading back to Big Sky. "Do you always think the worst of people? Or is this just because you don't like me, or something?"

"What?" she asked, sounding surprised. "I never said I didn't like you."

"Then why would you imply that I have some ulterior motive for looking for Grace?"

She sighed. "I didn't mean to cause a fight. I just…"

"You *just* don't trust *me*."

She leaned her head back against the truck's headrest. "I don't trust *anyone*."

He wasn't sure how to respond to that kind of blanket statement. He didn't wholeheartedly agree with her sentiment, but he could understand how and why she could come to feel that way. "Not all people are bad."

April nodded. "I don't think people ever want to be *bad*. At least, not usually. I think that people, in general, only do things when there is some kind of personal gain. No one does anything completely unselfishly."

He tried not to be offended as he thought about the thousands of hours he had spent in meetings, in training and actively volunteering to find those—like her—who needed help the most. "What about you? Why do you work with these kids? Are you saying that you are selfishly motivated in taking them out on activities?"

"First, I get paid," she said, putting up a finger like she was going to make a long list in her argument against not only him but herself as well. "Second, I enjoy them. And third, I like to think I can make a difference."

"How is enjoying your job selfish?"

"I love helping them. *I do*."

He tapped on the steering wheel. "Fair, but why?"

She tilted her head as though she was thinking, and her subtle little look of concentration made him want to stare. He had thought her naturally pretty before, but now all he could think about was how stunning she truly was in the way her blue eyes sparkled in the sun. There was a scratch on her chin that he had been staring at since he'd first found her on the mountain. Like the bruise around her eye, it appeared to be in the healing process, and it would likely be gone within a few days.

It was strange, but he would miss that little mark. He'd come to see the slight imperfection as much a part of her as the color of her eyes.

"I live just down there," she said, after they'd been driving for a bit. She pointed at the next road to their right. "If you want to swing by, I could use clean clothes and some gear."

"You got it," he said, pulling down the road.

He parked in the lot of the apartment complex next to a nineties-model, burgundy Chevy Caprice. The back window of the car was covered in a black plastic trash bag and secured with tape.

The place was made up of what looked like small units; parked in front of most were beat-up cars. Big Sky was made up of three types of people, the few and far between locals, the poor ski bums who worked hard in the summer to save up so they could ski all winter, and those with second homes who lived off trust funds and bonds. Just like him, April was definitely not a member of the latter.

"It's not much," she said, her face taking on a look of shame.

"Hey, you have a place to call your own," he said, trying to make her feel better. "You know as well as I do that around here a lot of people live in their cars."

She nodded, perking up slightly. "Did you hear that many business owners are complaining they can't find workers who will stay?" She guffawed. "I mean, how can they? No one can afford to live here on the wages most places are paying."

The thought made him think of Grace. What if she was out there, sleeping in one of the cars or campers that were parked in the woods and at every little pullout along the side of the road? What if someone was keeping her hostage?

"You can wait here," she said, stepping out of his pickup and closing the door before he had time to argue.

He wished he could tell her that she had nothing to be embarrassed about, truly. He didn't judge someone based on where they lived in this community. He judged people on their actions and the character they exhibited. Criminals and saints existed in every income bracket.

She rushed up to the first-floor apartment and slipped inside. It didn't take her long to come out carrying a small canvas bag that had had "Hike or Die" emblazoned on its side—he tried not to think about the irony.

His phone pinged with a message from his buddy, Jim Hagen, the fire marshal at the department. He clicked on it. Looks like we have a possible arson at the south end of town. All units are being called.

Do you have enough guys? he responded, watching as April came rushing toward his truck.

He had today and tomorrow off but he couldn't just leave her now, not with Grace still missing. If he bagged, she would never forgive him even if it was to go to work. Sure, she would tell him she knew that he had a job to do and a life outside what was happening in hers, but in the back of her mind she would feel abandoned. If he wanted to remain her friend—if that's what they even were—there would be no coming back from that kind of disappointment and hurt.

Yep, we're all set, Jim answered.

He put his phone face down on the console. April hopped into the pickup next to him and clicked her belt into place. "I think we should start looking for Grace at her best friend's house. Summer and a couple of her friends have an apartment not even that far from here." She took out her phone and opened Snapchat to see if Summer had a public account. "Yeah, according to this, Summer is a few blocks away. We can probably catch her."

He couldn't stand how invasive social media was in teens' lives without them even realizing the anonymity and freedoms they were giving up being a part of the "in crowd." As a kid, his parents had rarely known where he'd actually been, but in that ability to get lost to the world, he'd found who he truly was and had had the freedom to make choices that helped shape him into the man he was today.

Or maybe he was just old and stuck in the recursive and muddled loop of nostalgia.

When had thirty-two meant someone was old?

Then again, when he was running up the stairs and carrying hose in their training tower, he definitely felt his age.

"Yeah?" April asked, pulling him out of his negative self-talk.

"Good a spot as any to start," he said. "Did Grace have a boyfriend?"

She shrugged. "She had been hanging out with Andrew, but she and I didn't have the kind of relationship where she would have opened up about that kind of thing with me." She paused. "I wish we would have. That's what most of these kids need—a safe place and a mentor to help them navigate life—but it takes an event to form a bond."

He pulled out of the parking lot and drove in the direction she pointed.

Big Sky was a charming little town, tucked into the bottom of the ski hill. As they came to a stop at the sign at the end of the block, he spotted Mr. Crowly from the grocery store chatting with Sean's ex-girlfriend Persephone Samson. Mr. Crowly waved, but Persephone did her best impression of being blind. He couldn't blame her, especially after everything between them had ended so badly—and with too many fireworks.

April waved at Mr. Crowly. Thankfully, April didn't mention his most recent ex, but he didn't know if it was because she didn't know about his former relationship, or if she was kind enough not to mention it. Then again, she seemed to barely remember him from high school.

He pressed on the gas, only too happy to leave part of his past in the rearview mirror.

While he didn't know everyone in this town, he could confidently say that he knew everyone through one degree of separation. With that kind of accessibility and social media, it was like living in a fishbowl. The insularity made it almost impressive that Grace could have disappeared—he doubted she could have done it without some kind of help, but no one had stepped forward with any knowledge as to the girl's whereabouts.

The deputy in charge of her case had dotted all the *i*'s and crossed all the *t*'s in looking for her—and it didn't sound like they had found anything to make them think criminal or nefarious activities had taken place. From the coffee talk, the deputy seemed to be leaning toward thinking Grace had merely skipped town.

He wouldn't have blamed her if she had.

But he wished she *had* given someone some insights into why and where she was going.

Even in this small town, human trafficking was a concern. Several girls had snuck away and caught flights in Bozeman and headed toward the big cities, only to be later found on degenerate websites selling their bodies. One had even been murdered in the underground tunnels of Las Vegas.

"So…" April started. "Do you want to tell me why that woman back there with Mr. Crowly acted so weird?"

He sighed. "You noticed, huh?" He wished she hadn't.

"I think that any adult woman would have noticed the cold shoulder you just received. Did you hit it and quit it, or never give her a chance?" She sent him a cute, understanding smile.

He returned her smile, but he could feel the pain in his. "Boy, you just shoot from the hip, don't you?"

"Straight for the heart." She reached over with her casted arm and took hold of his hand, which rested on the console next to his phone. He moved his fingers up, wrapping her fingers with his. The action was so unexpected, that it made his heart sputter.

"I'm sorry," she continued.

"It's cliché, but everything happens for a reason." He glanced down at their hands and then gave her a squeeze.

She smiled. "Right now, I'm more thankful than ever in knowing that's true."

Chapter Six

April hadn't meant to slip her hand into his, but now she was glad she had taken the risk. Part of her problem was that she'd always allowed her mouth to get her in trouble— though her parents would have argued it wasn't just her mouth. She'd always been strong-willed and a Hell-yes girl, and that hadn't changed as she'd grown older.

Her impulsiveness had been a gift as much as it had been a burden, and thankfully this time it had worked in her favor. She could have stared at Sean forever. He was so handsome, and she'd be lying if she didn't have a thing for men in uniforms. Add the fact that he'd saved her *and* was a fireman... well, her personal restraint never stood a chance.

Unfortunately, this moment couldn't last. On Snapchat, Summer's blonde Bitmoji was quickly approaching. April pulled her fingers from his as she clicked on her phone. Sean then clasped his hands, making her wonder if he was questioning their brief touch.

As they neared, she spotted the teenager sitting out on the porch of her rental, vaping. She was standing with five other newly minted adults, none of whom looked overly happy about their arrival.

Sean parked across the street, and as they approached, she spotted the telltale movements of kids hiding beers.

Lucky for them, she wasn't there to be a voice of reason or run interference.

"Hey, Summer," she said, giving the girl a slight wave. "How's it going?"

Summer looked at the boy who was standing closest to her, like he was in control of her responding or not. April remembered those days when she'd ran second to a boy, but far from fondly.

The kid gave her a small nod and the girl turned back. "We're doin' okay, April. Who's the guy?"

"He's a friend," she said, not feeling the need to give the girl any real room for judgment until she could get a better feel for what she was walking into. "Did you hear about what happened up there on the hill?"

"Yeah," Summer said, a furious expression peppering her features. "I heard you screwed up and nearly got my best friend killed."

Anger pooled in April's belly, but she reminded herself that she was the reason they had been on the mountain in the first place. In so many ways, what had happened up there had been her fault and her responsibility.

"I am sorrier than you know about what happened," she said, lifting her cast slightly so they could see the evidence that she, too, hadn't come away unscathed, though her black eye had probably already done the trick.

Summer sniffed. The kids who'd been standing with her turned and escaped the storm as they headed inside. The only one remaining was the boy whom she'd been looking to for permission.

April stepped up onto the porch, Sean tailing her. "Did you happen to see or hear from Grace since it happened?"

"That's exactly what the cops asked the other day."

"And?"

"I told them exactly what I'm gonna tell you. Grace ain't been here."

April nodded. *So, we're going to play the twenty-questions game. So be it.*

"You know Grace and I had been hanging out for the last six months or so, pretty solid," April started, giving Sean a look like there was some secret that they shared.

Sean nodded, playing along.

"And?" Summer asked, taking a long drag off the vape pen. "She told me something about you… Things I bet you wouldn't want your little boy toy there hearing about—you know *exactly* who I'm talking about." She smirked.

"Whatever." She hated how much she sounded like a teenager as she thought about her ex, Damon.

"Funny thing, I guess Grace was right," she said. "You do seem to get more men than the average woman." She nudged her chin in the direction of Sean, but she clearly was also talking about Damon.

"Do you really think you should be shaming anyone?" April looked at the boy beside the girl and at the door where the rest of her squad had disappeared. "From what I see here, you have your choice of guys. You're having fun, and I don't begrudge you for it for a second. Have fun while you can."

The girl opened her mouth like she wanted to snark back but couldn't run with anything as there was no real condemnation.

"Look, *lady*," the guy standing beside Summer said, "you don't need to be coming here and starting a fight. The girl you're looking for ain't here. If what you're sayin' is true and she's been running with you for months, then she better be thinking twice before coming around, too."

"I wasn't trying to start anything. I just needed to know that she wasn't here, for sure."

Summer rolled her eyes. "You can't think you would get me to roll over when it comes to Grace."

"Oh?" April quirked a brow.

"Well, Grace is more than just a friend to me. She's almost a sister," Summer said.

Sean stepped up beside April. "If she's more like a sister, then we all know damned well that she has called you at the very least." He leaned against the post. "Grace isn't in any kind of trouble. We just need to know that she is okay and accounted for. So, if you've spoken to her…at least tell us and we can stop looking for her."

"We just need to know she's safe," April added.

There was a long pause, and Summer took another drag off her pink vape pen. She exhaled, and the air around April filled with the strange scent of cotton candy. If the girl was trying to come off as hard-edged, smoking something that smelled like sugar wasn't her best choice.

"Here's the deal," Summer started. "I ain't one to rat on my friend."

"So, you have spoken to her?"

"Last I heard, there was something going on with her foster parents. That was before your little hike. Since then, I ain't heard from her." Summer took another pull off the pen.

April stared at the girl, weighing her expression to tell if Summer was lying or telling the truth. Grace had offhandedly mentioned something to her about her foster family, something about them going on vacation.

"What do you mean, *something going on*?" Sean asked. "What was happening with her family?"

Summer's watchdog snarled at Sean's attempt to speak to her. "Look, man—"

The girl put a hand up, silencing her pet. "First, to call those adults *her family* is one hell of a stretch. They give her a roof over her head, and sometimes that is even hit or miss. Before she went to the Springs, she was spending a lot of nights over here with us. I even had to ask her to start chipping in on rent, but she decided to sign up with your camp instead."

"Bunch of good that did her," the watchdog snapped.

"Listen up, bucko…" Sean snarled back. "We are trying to help your friend here, and if you were as smart as you think you are, you'd be bending over backward to help us—that is, if Grace really was your friend, at all."

In the blink of an eye, the watchdog's fist was flying through the air. April let out a yelp as the kid's fist nearly connected with Sean's jaw. Instead, Sean grabbed his wrist and deftly maneuvered it behind the kid's back in an arm bar hold. He flipped his wrist back and the kid bent over in pain.

"What in the hell were you thinking, bucko?" Sean growled. "You may be able to take some fifteen-year-old idiot behind the football bleachers, but you're out of depths with me."

"Sean, stop." April shook her head. "Let's go, before someone calls the cops."

He turned back to the young guy he'd pinned. "You going to try something, again?"

The kid shook his head, tears in his eyes.

"Let him go," April ordered.

Sean dropped his arm. "I hope you learned something here, today. Don't mess with the old guy, kid, experience always wins."

Chapter Seven

Sean hadn't intended on things going as they had back at the adolescent tenement. At least he hadn't let the guy get the drop on him or he would have never let himself live it down. Ever since they'd left, April had been silent, and the tension rested between them like a boulder.

"So, you think we should head over to Grace's foster home?" he asked, knowing full well the police had already been there and there wasn't a chance in hell that Grace would go there to seek solace.

"Maybe you should take me back to my apartment," she said, pointing in the direction from which they'd come.

He chewed at the inside of his lip. "Look, I'm sorry about what happened. I didn't mean for things to go sideways like that. The kid was just—"

"Being a kid," she said, stopping him from saying what he really thought about the arrogant snotbag. "You need to realize that he and Summer are very much like the kids I work with at Sulphur Springs. They all have a chip on their shoulder. Your putting them in holds and getting in fistfights doesn't help in my attempts to prove to them that the world, and the adults in it, aren't their enemies."

"You are being idealistic," he countered, not meaning to start a fight, but unable to hold his tongue. "The world isn't filled with butterflies and rainbows. These kids know that better than anyone. Unfortunately, they are the ones who've had struggle to raise themselves, were indoctrinated into the underbelly of this society from an early age. You can fake it all you want, but people can't be trusted."

She jerked and turned to face him from the passenger's seat of his pickup. "Did you forget who you are talking to? Where I've come from? I thought you knew all about me. All about the girl I was in high school. I thought that's why you pitied me."

He scowled. "First, I don't pity you. Second, we talked about our high school years—they're not a time in either of our lives that we have to dig into. I know you had a hard time back then, but you aren't the only one with a past."

"Oh, really? Did your first love *die*? Did you have to give birth to the baby the two of you created all alone? Hand the little girl off to a stranger? Did you have to give away a part of yourself and the person you loved?"

He slowed down the pickup and pulled over to the side of the road near a small restaurant. It had a Closed sign in the window, which had faded with sun and age. He stared at its chipped edges as he tried to find the right words. For years, he had been carrying his secret…a secret that would have more of an impact on her than he'd realized, until now.

She sat back in her seat, sinking into it slightly. "I had to say goodbye to the two people I loved the most in this world all in the same year—Cameron and my baby, Ann. Ann was his mother's name," she said slowly.

It was a story he hadn't known and it was breaking his heart.

He wasn't ready to open up, to tell her his truth…not now.

"You don't know how sorry I am that you have gone

through all that." He pulled back onto the road. "I hate the fact that anyone should have to face such a thing alone... That's why I wanted to be a first responder. First, as a fire-fighter and second, as a volunteer for SAR."

"You are an anomaly. Everyone says they want to help, but then when it comes right down to it, no one shows up when you need them the most."

Her words drove into him, cutting him to pieces. He couldn't tell her all the reasons he'd been called to public service. If he did, it was likely that she would never speak to him again. There was no doubt in his mind that she would hate him, at the very least.

"Grace's home...it's just a few blocks down here," April said, pointing south. "Her foster parents rent a place."

"What do they do for a living?" Sean asked.

"Grace never really spoke about it, but from what I managed to glean, they both worked for the Spanish Peaks Restaurant. He as a chef, and she as a waitress. They don't seem to keep jobs for long, though."

"They're unreliable?" He felt stupid asking, but any number of things could have impacted their inability to maintain employment.

"I think that in this case, they aren't the best caregivers, or employees. However, I don't know them well enough at a personal level to say anything."

In the distance, a tendril of smoke rose into the sky. The site made his breath catch in his throat. This time of year, it was legal to burn slash outside town, but there was too much of the black billowing smoke to make him think that this was some little camp- or brushfire. Trying to keep his eyes on the road, he took out his phone. He pulled up his text messages, and he sent a quick one off to his buddy for the address of their active callout.

He pressed the gas pedal down harder as something in his gut made him wonder if the fire was somehow related to the missing girl.

Sirens were piercing the air as he approached a small duplex. Flames licked up the side of the building. The original color of the place looked to be beige, but now was mostly charred. Black, tarry smoke billowed out from the second-floor windows. At the far side of the building, red and orange flames were pouring out of the top of the window and meeting the fire crackling on the outside the structure.

The place had to have been burning for at least an hour as it was totally engulfed. Hopefully, if there had been people or animals inside, they had safely made it out.

Jim stood beside engine #406 talking on his phone. He waved at him as they rolled up to a stop on the other side of the street. There were people standing all over, rubbernecking and talking. Three different sheriff's deputies were patrolling the area, talking to what looked like several of the neighbors as well as managing crowd control.

"Is this Grace's foster family's place?" he asked.

"I think so, but…" April picked up her phone and tapped for a few seconds. "Yeah…it is." She sounded breathless.

His stomach roiled. "You don't think that Grace was in there, do you?"

She shook her head. "I hope with every part of my soul that she wasn't—Grace has and will continue to be a survivor."

APRIL'S HAIR FELL around her face and stuck at her temples. The fire was in a full roar now, even though the firefighters had been throwing water at it for an hour or more. Sean was safely away from the fire and was manning a hose from the second firetruck, and his T-shirt was sticking to his back, dark with pools of perspiration.

She had no idea how long they had been here, but since she'd arrived and from what she'd overheard, none of the firefighters had been able to venture back inside thanks to the intense heat and instability of the structure. However, the team who'd gone in earlier was now standing behind the first firetruck talking.

She didn't want to bother them and ask more questions, as they all looked exhausted and were drenched with sweat thanks to the heat of the fire and the seventy-degree weather. The man nearest to her was dark-haired and built like a muscle magazine cover model, and for a moment she could totally understand why most women found firefighters the sexiest thing on this planet.

There were two women across the street, both likely in their midthirties, who were tittering and giggling as they stared at the firemen. The women could have any one of them they wanted. That was, until the brunette pointed in the direction of Sean, who was moving the spray of water toward the second-floor window at the center of the building.

Her anger flared like a fire's hotspot. No. He was out of bounds.

As much as she wanted to march her butt across the street and tell the women to get back into their houses and quit objectifying what was hers, she restrained herself and simply made her way over to the resting firemen. Though she would have rather gone over to Sean and marked her territory, this would work as a close second in her attempts to let the women know that she was the one in the power position.

As she approached them, she realized how stupid she was being. First of all, she didn't want any of these men— Sean included. *I mean, it's not like holding hands meant we have anything beyond a friendship. Friends hold hands all the time—don't they?*

Second of all, she shouldn't have been thinking about the hot or not qualities of the cover-model-esque and sweaty men surrounding her. She needed to quell the lizard part of her brain that was sending her into the primal way of thinking, which involved chest pounding and clubs.

There were so many other things she should have been thinking about. Thankfully, no one had mentioned finding any signs that anyone had been in the house at the time of the fire.

"What's up?" Another fireman by the engine turned to her and sent her a sweltering smile that had nothing to do with the heat.

"Do you guys need anything?" she asked, doing her best not to send the women across the street a suck-on-that look as much as her ego wanted.

The blond smiled. "We're good. Sean said you're the woman he found on the mountain the other day. How's your arm doing?" he asked, motioning toward her cast.

She wasn't trying, but damn if his concern didn't make her thoughts move to Sean. Hopefully he wasn't watching and seeing she was talking to these ridiculously good-looking men. Then again, would he even realize how handsome they were? Or, for that matter, that she thought they were sexy?

Gah... I am a hot mess. She tried to keep her thoughts

from being read upon her features, but she could feel her cheeks warm. *I can think other men are sexy. I'm not in a relationship. I'm not spoken for. Besides, they didn't hold a candle to Sean. And damn it, I'm not dead.*

Dead. The word echoed through her.

"My arm's fine. A little sore, but I'm sure that's nothing in comparison to what you guys are feeling. I bet you're exhausted."

He sent her a sexy smile that made her step back.

Why did her best attempt to talk to these men sound like she was trying to hit on them? *All I'm missing is the hair flip and the vapors, and they would think I was vying for a husband. Maybe Summer and Grace are right... I have a problem when it comes to men.*

Stop being awkward, she told herself. *Stop. Being. Awkward.*

"Are you okay?" Blondie asked, frowning at her like he was concerned she was having some kind of stroke in front of him.

Come on, really? This couldn't have been the first time you've had a woman go full spastic in front of you, she wanted to say. Instead, she smiled. "I'm fine, sorry. I'm just really concerned. One of my campers from Sulphur Springs was supposed to be living in this duplex. Her name is Grace. She's sixteen."

The man's playful demeanor disappeared and was replaced with a look of gravity. "Sean told us a bit about the girl. We didn't see any evidence people were in the building when we went in, but that's not to say we couldn't have missed someone. Until the fire is contained and we can get back inside, I'm afraid I can't say anything for sure."

What if Grace had been inside? What if she had *caused*

the fire? "How long do you think it will take to get inside and look for possible remains?"

The blond man looked at his friend and then over at Sean, as though he wished she had put any one of the other men on the spot besides him. "You will have to talk to Sean, but I would say it will be at least a day or so."

"You won't know if someone died in this fire for at least a day? What about finding out the cause of the fire? Will that take a month?" she growled, trying and failing at not losing her temper. All she wanted to know was if the girl they were looking for was alive or dead at this point, and yet...*nothing*.

The man frowned and ran his hand over the back of his neck. The men he'd been standing with seemed to take a step back and the farthest from her actually turned away and made a show of going to the side of the engine and starting to work with a section of hose.

She was blaming the wrong person, but she couldn't help how desperate and powerless she felt. "I'm sorry, I didn't mean to come off like a jerk. I just…"

The blond man motioned for Sean, who was glancing over at them. "I'll go grab him for you. He can answer your questions better than I can." Before she could say anything else to try to make up for her rudeness, he nearly started jogging to get away from her. The women watching were probably eating up the men's retreat from her.

The blond took over the hose, relieving Sean, whose shoulder muscles were pulled tight against his shirt. As the man spoke to him, he glanced back over at her and there was a look of concern on his face. Sean was probably three steps ahead of her and thinking about Grace and her potential for being somehow linked to this fire—or, and she hoped not, how Grace was dead inside.

He wiped the back of his hand over his forehead and said something with a nod to the blond, then he made his way over. He walked slowly and deliberately toward her. Even from here, it was clear that there was something he didn't want to tell her.

"Is she dead?" she asked, terrified.

If Grace was gone, she'd never be able to forgive herself. April was supposed to be this girl's mentor and not only had she gotten her involved in a rockslide, but then she'd been unavailable in the hospital and now...

She grew nauseous.

Sean rubbed his left wrist, a sign that he was nervous. "Since we arrived, the deputies have been out here taking statements from the neighbors, as well as any other potential witnesses. Have any of them made their way over and chatted with you yet?"

The wave of nausea grew within, forcing her to try to swallow it down. "No. Why? What do they think happened?"

He took her by the hand. "Let's go sit in my pickup for a minute, so we can have some privacy while we talk."

She couldn't move her feet. "If there's something you know, something about Grace...you have to tell me right now. I can't... I *need* to know if you think she's dead."

As though he could tell that she was fighting within herself to remain in check, he gripped her hand tighter. "It's okay—I don't think she's dead. I think everything is going to be okay. Let's just go for a quick walk to the pickup."

She didn't love his attempt to mollify her, but at the same time she found some relief and comfort in his words. Everything would be fine. She had to trust him.

Silently, she let him lead her toward his pickup. He

opened the door and helped her inside before making his way over to the driver's side and getting in. As he did, the aroma of sweat and ash filled the small space.

He took in a long breath.

He was being so reticent in talking to her, but he'd told her everything was going to be fine. Why? "Was she inside?"

"I didn't think she was inside… I really didn't."

"Didn't?" He was speaking in past tense. Which meant only one thing…now he did believe she had been inside. "She's in there? You think she…*was*…inside?" she asked, struggling to come to terms with what she was saying.

"One of the neighbors believes she saw a teenage girl entering the house about ten minutes before the fire really took off."

"Did she see anyone leave?" April tried to remind herself to breathe. "You said you didn't think she was dead…"

"She didn't come out—at least, they didn't see her." He shook his head, concern filling his eyes. He reached over and took her hand with his. "I'm hoping that the woman was wrong. But the description she gave was consistent with that of Grace. Teenage girl. Green hair. And she believed the girl had a black eye. I think she slipped out before the fire took off. Ten minutes…that's probably how long she was in there."

Is he saying he thought Grace had set the fire?

She didn't know what to say, or how to feel. Grace wasn't likely to commit arson and she wasn't suicidal, at least not from what April knew or what she had managed to read from the girl.

"She…she has to still be alive."

He nodded, giving her a look as though he was taking it

easy on her. "She is probably alive, but there's talk Grace may have started the fire." Sean squeezed her hand.

"What?" April sank deeper into her seat. "No. That doesn't fit. She wouldn't do something like that."

He studied her, like he was trying to decide if she knew something about the girl he didn't and as he did, she wished she didn't have a rising feeling that she was wrong. This girl *did* come from a family that wasn't the best, and she had been in trouble before. There was no way to really say for sure that this troubled teen wouldn't have committed arson.

Almost as though he could read the thoughts on her face, he nodded. "Just because we want to assume the best of the people we care about doesn't mean they are actually worthy of you giving them the benefit of the doubt. Grace was...*is* troubled."

"There's no doubt about that." She started tapping her foot.

He glanced down at her nervous movement. "It's been a long day. How about you come over to my place?"

And just like that, her nervousness amplified.

Chapter Eight

Sean added the finishing touches to his best attempt at a charcuterie board. He barely paid attention as he placed the end of the cheese back in the fridge.

All he could think about was April and how he wanted to take her into his arms and tell her everything would be okay, but nothing he could say or do would help her get through this without more pain and disappointment. He hated that he had to be the one at the epicenter of this battle she was facing, one without any clear-cut answers. In fact, the only thing he knew with any certainty was he had played more of a role in the destruction of her life than he wanted to, or could, admit.

"Look, we don't know if Grace was inside the house. Maybe it wasn't her," he said, walking out of his kitchen while carrying her a plate of salami and cheese—the only thing he'd had in his fridge on this short notice. Having a guest wasn't something he'd prepared for.

"That's what I'm hoping. I just wish we had more answers." April turned in the recliner, and he handed her the plate and the glass of wine. The wine had been the five-buck-chuck stuff from the market at the corner; he'd bought it the last time he thought he had a possibility of bringing a woman back to his place. Which, come to think about it, had been more than six months ago. He was sure this kind of wine wasn't the type that got better with age.

He had beer in the fridge, but the last time he'd bought a woman a beer at Great Northern Bar, she'd turned up her nose at him like he'd somehow committed the worst crime on the planet. He hadn't wanted to offend April.

"I have my ringer on, and as soon as Jim finds anything of use, he will let us know."

She nodded and took a long drink from the wineglass he'd bought at the secondhand store. As she drank, he noticed the chip on the edge of the glass. He wasn't sure if he should say something. Thankfully, from the way she was putting the wine down, he doubted she would really notice or, if she did, that she would say anything.

"I hope you're okay with what I've got in the kitchen. We can order something in, too. I don't have a ton of stuff on hand, sorry. About all I have food-wise is cat food."

She waved him off as she drained the glass. "You're fine. Wait... You have a cat?"

He nodded. "He's a gray American shorthair and he's pretty shy, but he is around here someplace. He doesn't usually come out unless it's really quiet."

"I like him already," she said with a smile. "I hope he's okay with me being here. And I hope you know how much I appreciate you having me over. I didn't feel like going back to my place and staring at the walls until we heard something."

"At least they have gotten the fire completely under control," he said, looking at his watch. It was nearly midnight. It had been the longest day, yet the shortest as she had been by his side. It was crazy how fast time seemed to move when they were together.

"If he calls when I'm sleeping, don't worry about waking me up. I'm a light sleeper. But he isn't going to work overnight anyway, right? He has to wait for things to cool down, first."

He nodded. "And I'm the opposite. Unless you have an alarm going off or there's smoke in the air, there isn't much of a chance of waking me up." He smiled at the thought of getting to see her when she was sleeping.

The only thing that could have made it better was if he was holding her in his arms.

She was so beautiful.

She smiled up at him. "What if I want to wake you up? If I need something?"

He wasn't sure, but he could have sworn there was a flirtatious lilt to her voice as she spoke.

"I'm at your mercy."

If only he was better at reading between the lines with women. He absolutely sucked at seeing when a woman was flirting with him. His ex used to laugh at him when they were out in public and women would talk to him. He'd think they were being nice, and she would tease him…and then be furious with him by the end of the night. Her shift from laughter to fury always made him wonder if it wasn't actually that he was being hit on or if she was just looking for reasons to fight. To this day, he wasn't sure.

He sat down on the couch next to April and turned on the television, putting on *Hot in Cleveland*. He'd not watched it, but he'd heard it was funny from Cindy.

As the show played in the background, his gaze kept slipping over toward April. Her blond hair had fallen into her face, and a piece was gently tracing the curve of her cheek—exactly where he would have given anything to trace his finger.

She laughed as she watched the show, and his heart lightened with her sound. It was a relief to hear her laugh. He couldn't recall hearing that sound from her before, and it was addictive.

She turned slightly, catching his eyes as he stared at her. "I love Betty White. She is so funny." She popped a piece of cheese into her mouth, making his gaze move to her lips. She licked them, and he tried to control his desire to feel those lips pressed against his.

He couldn't remember a time he had ever wanted a woman more. He wanted to reach across the couch and take her into his arms and make her forget about everything but him and this moment. Yet, how could he kiss her when there was such a heavy secret between them?

Maybe a kiss could be some kind of remedy. Maybe not for the secret, but at least it could take away some of the stresses they were both feeling. It wouldn't hurt their search. They were merely both volunteering. Aside from his own inadequacies and the nature of the situation that had brought them together, there was nothing standing in their way when it came to taking things a step further.

Betty White said something about breaking a hip, and April let out a long laugh. It was too much. He moved closer to her. "Do you need another glass of wine?"

She nodded, reaching over and grabbing her glass. "That would be great. It's been such a long day."

As he moved for the glass, their fingers grazed against each other, and her gaze snapped over to him. There was a soft smile on her lips, and she looked down at their touching fingers and then back up at him. Her blue eyes caught the light of the lamp on the side of the couch behind him. "I…" she said, "I think you should get a glass, too."

He nodded, but as he moved to get up, she shot to her feet. "Do you want anything else?" she asked, her words coming fast as though she was nervous.

He wanted her, but he didn't know if he could dare to say such a thing aloud. "Wine is good." *But* you *would be better*.

She nearly sprinted into the kitchen, and he retreated to the far corner of the couch. He had screwed up. Maybe she was feeling unnerved by their being so close together and alone.

April's phone buzzed on the side table.

Though he knew he shouldn't, he was tempted to take a look at who was trying to get ahold of her.

Her phone buzzed again.

His stomach tightened as he leaned back into his seat on the couch. He didn't have any right to know who was trying to get in touch with her—that was, unless it had to do with the search.

"April," he called, getting to his feet and trying his damnedest not to peek at the screen as it buzzed again. He glanced down and spotted a man's pic looking up at him with the name "Damon." The guy looked like a jerk. He had a beard and a big, dumb smile that Sean would want to punch off the dude if he saw him in person.

He had to be the guy Summer had mentioned earlier.

He flopped back down on the couch. She should have told him that she had a boyfriend. Maybe that was why she had seemed so uncomfortable with him—she didn't want to tell him that she was taken. Or maybe she was just looking for a place to stay where she wouldn't have to be alone—maybe Damon was out of town for the night or something.

He gritted his teeth so hard that his jaw cramped.

After a few minutes, she returned from the kitchen, two beers in her hand. She handed him one. "I hope you don't mind that I made a switch. I'm not much of a wine drinker."

He smiled at her. "What's mine is yours. Plus I'm sure that wine was terrible."

She laughed as she sat down on the couch beside him. "I'm not going to say that it tasted like feet, but I'm pretty sure I got a big toe in my glass. Though…" she said, taking a drink of her beer, "it didn't really slow me down. I figure having a couple glasses must be as effective for my arm as taking a couple painkillers."

Her phone buzzed and, when she picked it up, he saw the same name as earlier. She slammed her phone down on the couch beside her and shoved it violently under her leg.

"You can answer that, if you need to." He motioned toward the phone she'd been trying to hide.

"No. I'm good," she said, not giving him any more information than he already knew.

He didn't like it. "He called when you were grabbing drinks, too."

"Oh," she said, touching the phone under her leg as it buzzed again. "Well, he doesn't need to talk to me now… or ever."

"So, that's not your boyfriend?" he asked, hope dulling some of the sharp edges of the jealousy he had been feeling.

She delicately nibbled on her lip. "We have hung out a few times, but the guy just doesn't know how to take a hint."

He wasn't sure what that was supposed to mean. "Does that mean he's still a part of your life?"

She shrugged. "I haven't been out with him for a few months, but we work together, and he thinks it's fine if he calls all the time. If I try to block him, he just changes his number. It's gotten ridiculous."

"Hold up…" He paused, putting down his beer on the table next to him. "This guy is *harassing* you?" His anger flared. "Has he *hurt* you?" The words rang funny in his ears as he heard himself speak and try to judge anyone else for doing her harm, when harm was what he had brought most of to her life.

He had to tell her the truth…*eventually*.

"The guy is pathetic. He knows I don't want to see him again, but he always manages to weasel his way back into my life. He wears me down with the constant phone calls and texts. It's easier to give one-word responses than to have him keep badgering me."

"April…" he said, surprised by her situation, "that's called stalking. Have you talked to anyone? A lawyer?"

She shook her head. "It's not that bad. He hasn't threatened me or anything. He just is *persistent*. And there are times at work when I *have* to talk to him about things."

She could call it anything she wanted, but if he met the guy, he would want to punch Damon's teeth down his throat. Damon, coworker or not, was a letch.

Her phone started buzzing again. "Do you really want him to stop calling you?" he asked.

Some of the color drained from her face. "I do. Why?"

"If you want, I will talk to him and handle this. Just hand me your phone." He extended his hand.

"I…I can handle him. It's just—"

He didn't doubt she was telling him the truth about the man, not from the look on her face whenever that phone buzzed, but he was surprised she didn't want him to help. "You can count on me to protect you. It's what I do."

"I hope you don't think that I'm some kind of damsel in distress." She chewed on her lip, harder, as she pulled her phone out and looked down at the screen.

"You've needed help this week, and there is nothing wrong with that. We all have moments in our lives when we have to count on other people to help us get through. Just think of this as me helping you out of another rock-slide…just this time the rock is this piece of work."

She handed her phone over. "I don't think he's going to listen to you. He definitely hasn't been listening to me."

"What is there to lose?" He slid the green dial on the phone, answering. "Hello?" It sounded like a low, dangerous growl.

"Who is this?" the guy on the other end of the line asked. "Where's April?"

His lip quivered as he tried to control his snarl. "April is busy."

"Give her the phone. I need to talk to her about work."

"Damon, she doesn't want to talk to you…not now and not ever. In fact, if you keep harassing her, you'll have to deal with me, and you don't want that, trust me."

The guy laughed. "Boy, she has you curled around her finger…doesn't she? Listen here, she's mine and she's always going to be mine. She may play with you and tell you she loves you, but I'm the one she's always thinking about."

"She's always thinking about you because you are scaring her." He looked over at April, who had started to pace beside the couch. "Is that how you achieve power over women? By breaking them down until they feel like they have to talk? Yeah, you're a big man."

"Screw you," the guy said. "You have no idea what damage you just caused." He hung up the phone.

"Wait…" But it was too late, the phone line was dead.

As Sean put the phone down, fear filled him—not that he could admit that to April. He had promised he would help her, but now he was concerned he done exactly the opposite.

April had been right, this guy was a real piece of work.

She looked over at him with a questioning expression.

"I think you should get yourself a new cell number tomorrow." He put the phone down on the table. "In the meantime, you need to tell me more about this guy. Did he know that you were hurt on the mountain? Where was he when you were in the hospital?"

"I'm sure he heard about the accident." She took her phone and shoved it under her leg. "He's another one of the counselors at the camp."

"What? You said you worked with him, but I didn't think—" He couldn't believe that her admission hadn't sunken in until now. Of course, the guy was a counselor. "How is this guy able to work with kids?"

"Everyone has their quirks," she said, staring down at the edge of the couch like it held some kind of answers.

"Stalking and harassing a woman isn't a *quirk*, it's illegal."

"He's obnoxious and rude, but—"

"No, April. Don't minimize this. You and I both know this guy is a problem, that he shouldn't be around you or children. Have you told your bosses about him?"

She shook her head. "They have enough on their plates. It was my mistake for thinking I could date someone there."

"No, none of this is your fault."

She stared at the ground. "He hasn't done anything to

harm the kids. As for me, he's harmless. He just wants my attention."

"Is he, though?"

She finally looked up and sent him a forced smile. "I can't help it if I'm so desirable that men refuse to let me slip through their fingers." She tried to laugh, but the sound was awkward and strangled. She reached over and touched the back of his hand. "Seriously, though, let's not talk about him. There're more important things we could be focusing on."

He didn't like her deflection, but he didn't want to make her any more uncomfortable than she already was. "Grace?" He moved his hand over hers.

"I know I should say yes, but until we know what happened with the fire..." She edged closer to him. "I was thinking we could relax."

He could think of any number of things he wanted to do right now, most involving kicking her ex's ass, but he tried to stuff down the feelings. Just because he wanted to protect her and keep her safe didn't mean it was what she needed.

His gaze moved to her hot pink cast. "I bet you are exhausted. You want to watch a movie or something? You need to rest so you can heal."

She nodded, and there was a tiredness in her eyes he hadn't even noticed until this moment. The kind that came more from a weary soul than the late hour. He'd seen it so many times when he'd been called to fires and he'd spoken to homeowners or survivors.

If only there was something else he could do to make her forget. Recently, he'd heard a concept about moving through pain. He couldn't remember it exactly, but from what he remembered it was basically the philosophy that everyone experienced pain—varying levels, but pain, nonetheless. What helped people keep hoping were what they called moments of "glimmer." Glimmer were small moments in time in which the heart lifted, and true happiness or relief could be found.

For him, a single glimmer in the heaviest of darkness could do more help than any words of consolation or comfort. His thoughts moved to the day he'd watched Cameron, April's former boyfriend, die on the side of the road. He had been holding his friend when Cameron had taken his last breath. It had taken Sean years to recover. In fact, there were days that the memory swept back into his life and threatened to steal his soul once again.

He'd been lost and was considering ending his life in some twisted tribute and apology; that was, until he'd found a glimmer. It had come when he'd been working as a custodian at the local high school a month after he graduated. It was the night shift, and he'd been cleaning in the shop area, thinking about Cameron and the car accident, when he'd heard a mewing come from the corner. He tracked down the sound and in an old, rusted-out engine cylinder was a tiny kitten. Its eyes weren't even open, and it had appeared to be no more than a few days old.

The thing had been tiny. He'd never seen anything so newly born and the creature had terrified him at first. He hadn't had a clue how to take care of the animal. Yet, he'd stayed near it. He'd opened the shop door slightly, waiting for the mother cat to come in and retrieve it, but she never came. After spending the night on the floor of the auto shop classroom, he'd left. It had been the weekend, but that little kitten had haunted him the second he'd gotten home.

Six hours later, with kitten formula and strict instructions on how to care for a newborn, he returned. The kitten hadn't moved, and he'd wrapped it in a towel and brought it to a vet's office, and then finally home with him. He nursed it every few hours. When the baby had perked up and started to open its eyes, he'd finally decided to name it Piston.

It was silly to admit, and he wouldn't say it aloud, but that old cat had saved his life.

Now, what April needed most was a glimmer.

Chapter Nine

April scooched closer to Sean on the couch. As sore as she was feeling, he was the one who looked to be in the most pain. She couldn't make sense of the expression on his face. At first thought, she would have assumed his discomfort was caused by the situation with Grace, but that look hadn't shown up until after Damon had called and interrupted their night.

She really did hate that guy.

Her hand moved into his and Sean smiled over at her, the pained look in his eyes finally disappearing. "Are you okay?" he asked. "Warm enough? I think I have a blanket around here somewhere if you need something."

"I know this sounds strange," she said, wishing she was better at the game she was about to try to play.

"What?" he asked, as an advertisement played on the television between scenes of *Hot in Cleveland*.

"It's been a really long day...actually, you can call it a week." She looked at his chest, yearning for his touch. "I could use a snuggle."

Though she was aware she was playing with fire in wanting to be so close and for him to touch her, she couldn't resist the desire. She needed to be held, to be touched by someone who would keep her safe—at least, in this moment.

He nodded, his smile widening. He let go of her fingers and lifted his arm, opening up his chest. "Bring it in."

She moved in close and looked up at him. "This isn't too weird?"

"I want you to be comfortable. If this is what you need tonight, you got it." He cleared his throat. "And, if this is *all* you want… I respect that. This can be a onetime, see-a-need-fill-a-need kind of thing."

She appreciated the fact that he wasn't going to pressure her for something she wasn't sure she was ready for with him. Then again, he was so hot. If she had less going on in her life, and she wasn't in a dumpster fire phase, she would have jumped on this opportunity to spend the night with him as something more than friends. Yet, as she was getting older, she was coming to realize that while sex was fun, it led to more complications than comfort.

"Thank you, Sean." She laid her head against his chest.

"For what?" he asked, his words making his chest vibrate against her face and sending gentle shivers down her spine.

"Not trying to force anything. Saving me. Being you. Take your pick." She put her hand on his chest, hoping to feel the sweet vibrato of his voice on the palm of her hand.

"If you think you need to thank me, or that I've done anything to be thankful for, you need to hang out with a higher caliber of men."

She wrapped her fingers in the cotton of his shirt as his words filled her hand like gold flecks. If only she could keep them, him, and this moment, forever.

"You've done more than you know." Her thoughts moved to the moment she'd awakened to find him beside her after her accident. From the moment that fate had brought them back together, he had been saving her.

He put his hand on hers and held it tight. "I could say the same of you."

"All I've done is bring craziness into your life," she said, with a gentle laugh.

"Didn't you know, I'm an adrenaline junkie," he said, stroking her hand with his thumb. "Really, you've brought me everything I needed."

"If you stick with me, the one and probably only thing I can promise you with any certainty is that you will never be bored."

She thought about how different her life would have been if she hadn't dated Cameron in high school and had, instead, been with Sean. At the time, they hadn't run with the same crowds. He'd been a football player and class president, while she had been hanging out outside the Grange, a small bar on the outskirts of town that was notorious for serving underage girls.

It was strange to think that as differently as they had started life, they had still been brought back together and found this moment—even if it was only temporary.

She soaked in the feeling of his skin on hers. Her plaster-casted arm started to cramp as she laid against him. She needed to move her shoulder and get the pressure off her arm, but she didn't want to give in to the pain. Shifting, she tried to take some pressure of her broken arm.

"Are you okay?" he asked, sitting back slightly as if he could tell that she was hurting.

"It's my stupid arm," she said, moving it slightly between them.

"Here," he said, moving, "sit up a little."

Moving was the last thing she wanted to do. She was finally where she wanted to be—in his arms. She shook her head. "I'll be fine, really."

He sent her a little half smile, like he could tell what she was thinking. "We can go back to cuddling, I promise."

She sighed as he let go of her hand and she sat up. He stood. "I'll be right back, wait here."

The movie played over the fireplace on the wall as she tried to patiently wait for him to come back. After a few minutes, though, when he still hadn't returned, she got up from the couch and made her way down the hallway. "Sean, is everything okay?" she called, hoping she wasn't interrupting him on the phone or something.

He didn't answer.

She wasn't sure if she should keep looking for him, or if he had forgotten about her or fallen asleep and she should just tuck back into the couch for the night. At the far end of the hall, there was a closed door. She stopped at it, giving it a gentle tap.

"Come on in," he answered.

There was a little part of her that was excited to see what he was doing, and her thoughts moved to him lying on the bed, centerfold spread, and just waiting for her to find him. If he was naked and waiting, she wouldn't be able to say no to her devilishly handsome rescuer. On the other hand, he'd promised her things wouldn't head that way…but that didn't mean a girl couldn't hope.

She pushed open the door and she caught her breath.

He was still dressed, but he was perched on his elbow and lying on his side on the bed, and he was curled around a little gray tabby cat. "Oh…" she said, smiling at the sweet picture in front of her. "Who do we have here?"

"This is Piston," he said, the cat yawning as he gently

scratched behind his ears. "I rescued him when he was only a few days old."

She walked over to the bed and sat down beside the cat and Sean. "You told me you had a cat running around. You didn't tell me he was so handsome."

He stopped petting Piston and motioned for her to take over. She was happy to oblige, and as she stroked the cat, he moved and stretched, exposing his belly for rubs.

Sean looked surprised. "You know," he said, "I've had this boy for fourteen years, and I don't think he's ever let anyone else touch him."

"I've always had a thing for cats. You're not the first person to say something like that to me." She smiled.

"You must be an animal whisperer." He patted the pillow on the other side of the bed. The television was playing, and its sound was muffled as she lay down beside Piston and Sean.

As she petted the cat, cooing softly, there was something about the moment that made her thoughts move to what it would have been like to have a family. If she had kept her baby, if Cameron had lived, if her life had been different, this could have been hers. The thought threatened to steal away the joy in the moment, but she pushed away the yearning for a life missed.

She closed her eyes as she tried to feel nothing but the happiness in her heart.

APRIL'S EYES CLOSED and soon her chest was moving with the steady breaths of sleep. Sean smiled at the serenity in her face. For the first time since he'd found her, she finally looked at peace.

There was a strand of hair caught in the corner of her

mouth and he was tempted to reach over and fix it for her, but resisted the urge. She needed to rest. She needed to heal. Plus he needed to keep his hands off her. It had been so hard to resist the urge to kiss her ever since they had set foot in his house. She had been so vulnerable and stripped of all pretenses that had he been a lesser man, to take her into his arms and find respite in one another's naked body would have been easy. Yet, he had told her she didn't have to worry about an advance.

Now, he wished he hadn't given her such guarantees. He would have given his left eyetooth to simply kiss her—nothing more.

He carefully got out of bed. Piston peeled his eye open, squinting at him with an edge of annoyance, but then closed his eyes once again.

I get it, buddy, he thought. *If I was where you are, I wouldn't give up my spot, either.*

He moved to the doorway and looked back, taking in the scene on his bed for a long moment. He didn't want to be weird, but he could have watched them together all night. To see Piston so at home with this woman who meant more to him than she knew and was deeper into his heart with every passing hour, was incredible.

Going to his hall closet, he pulled out a blanket his grandmother had crocheted for him when he'd been a kid. It was blue and orange, and he'd slept with it into his teens and well past the point it was probably normal to keep childish things, but it had always been his favorite. It seemed only right that he'd use something that meant a great deal to him throughout his life to now keep April safe and warm. It was the least he could do.

He slipped back into the bedroom and gently placed

the blanket over her. She rustled slightly as he stepped to leave, and she moved her hand to his. His smile returned at the honest moment. She wanted him. He could feel it in the way her skin brushed against his.

Reaching up, he moved the wayward strand of hair from her lips. Like Piston had, she peered up at him and a sleepy smile came over her lips. "Kiss me good night."

She didn't need to ask him twice. Leaning over, he kissed the soft skin of her forehead, happy for any chance to press his lips against her. However, she lifted her chin, moving her lips to his. She reached up, placing her arm over his shoulder and pulling him closer to her and deeper into their kiss.

She tasted like beer, and he licked the tang from her lips. He could imagine that the rest of her body would likely taste just as delicious. He grew hard at the thought of taking her, all of her.

As he moved closer to her, Piston retreated from the bed, but not before throwing them a sideways glance.

He laughed at the cat before turning back to what he had been doing.

She moaned into his mouth, and he moved between her thighs. He traced the line of her jaw with his kisses and buried his face in her neck as his hunger raced through him.

"Sean." She whispered his name like it was a precious secret.

"Mmm?" He kissed the line of her collarbone.

"I want you," she said, pressing her fingers through his hair and gently tugging. "I want all of you."

He groaned as he grew impossibly harder, pressing painfully against the zipper of his jeans.

"I want you to make me forget…everything that has happened in the past."

Just like that, he was pulled out of his study of her body. He'd nearly forgotten about the hurt and pain he'd caused in her life, and now it had come slamming, fist-like into the center of his gut.

He couldn't have her…not until she knew his truth.

Chapter Ten

Sean had left the room so quickly last night that April was afraid to talk about what had happened and how she had frightened him away. In the long list of mistakes she had made in her life, his retreat from between her thighs had to be one of the worst.

Why had she opened her mouth and spoken her thoughts? If she had just shut up and let things progress, she wouldn't have woken up aching and more confused.

Instead, she'd messed everything up. If she hadn't asked him to kiss her…but she couldn't regret asking. Not that. That was the one thing she had done right last night.

As she walked out of his bedroom, Sean was up and working in the kitchen. It smelled like coffee and bacon and as she came in, he handed her a steaming mug. "Good morning," he said, sounding slightly sheepish.

He must have been feeling as awkward and confused as she was.

"Sorry I took over your bed last night," she offered, trying to dance around the real topic that was standing between them. "You know, I could have given you the bed."

"Oh, no," he said, turning away like he feared that she would read something on his face. "It was all yours. It can be as long as you want to stay here, by the way."

Even with his offer, he didn't turn to look at her. She wasn't about to grill him on the fine points, and whether or not "as long as you want" was a day or a lifetime.

She laughed at herself as she sipped on her piping-hot coffee. He even made coffee perfectly, cream and sugar included. It was a great man who met a woman with a cup upon waking. He really was a keeper.

He might have been right about her needing a higher caliber of men in her life—especially if this was the kind of treatment that was included.

"Piston stayed with me all night. I think he finally got up around five." She tried to make small talk without rubbing against the subject of his leaving.

"He must have heard me. I had to run and grab a few things at the store so I could make you breakfast." He smiled and set down a plate of eggs and bacon with toast in front of her. He grabbed a jar of grape jelly off the counter and popped open the lid.

"Thank you," she said, taking the jelly with a wide grin. "You went out of your way. I appreciate it." She didn't have the heart to tell him that she wasn't much of a breakfast eater. Besides, she wasn't going to turn down an opportunity like this.

He turned his back to her, and she watched his jeans stretch hard against his backside. She could have stared at that backside forever. He had to do at least a hundred squats a day to make it look that good.

"I wasn't sure how you took your eggs, or your coffee," he said, looking back at her over his shoulder. "Is everything to your liking?"

In all my life, I don't think I've ever had a guy make me

breakfast. Or care how I like my eggs, for that matter, she thought.

She was loving the fact that she was being spoiled, but at the same time he was ruining her for all future men. If she started to get used to this level of care and consideration, she wasn't sure she would ever be able to go back to a hit-it-and-quit-it type of relationship. *Er, rather, a situationship.*

"Everything is perfect." The statement was far more inclusive than she'd intended, but she didn't care if he inferred the true meaning of her words.

He grabbed a second plate for himself and dished it up. Sitting down next to her, he took a long sip of his black coffee.

"Did you have to buy everything for this breakfast this morning, or did you have a few things on hand?"

"No..." He gave her a sheepish grin. "I had a canister of coffee."

"But you had to buy everything else?" she asked.

"It wasn't a big deal. I needed to stock up. Piston is *super needy*." He laughed, and the sound caressed her like a hand and made goose bumps raise on her arms.

That's new. She put her hand over her arm, inadvertently attempting to cover what he could make her feel with just his voice.

He couldn't know the power he held over her. If he did, he would be able to get away with darn near anything.

Popping a piece of toast in her mouth, she chewed as he turned to look at her. "So...about last night."

If she didn't know better, she would have thought he'd picked this exact moment, that was, with her mouth full, to bring this up.

"Mmm-hmm," she mumbled, trying to chew faster.

"I hope you know how much I wanted you…and to take things further." He ran his hand over the back of his neck as if he was deeply uncomfortable.

She swallowed. "But?"

There was always a *but*.

"There's something I have to tell you…" He paused as he stared down at his plate. "I'm worried you may not take it well. But please promise to hear me out."

All of a sudden, all desire to eat left her. "Okay… What did you *do*? Did something happen to Grace? Did they find her?" Her stomach roiled.

He put his hands up. "No. No. It has nothing to do with Grace. In fact, it happened a long time ago."

She relaxed a little and reminded herself to take a breath.

"Do you remember the night that Cameron died?" he asked.

Of course she remembered that night. It had been two weeks after she'd told him about her positive pregnancy test. He'd promised her they were going to spend together forever, and he would marry her and take care of their baby. They'd had two years left in high school before they would graduate. And yet, in the blink of an eye and a single phone call later, he was gone and with him so were her dreams of a future.

"Yes," she said simply.

"I was there."

Her whole body jerked. "What do you mean *you were there*? He was the only one in the car that night." She stared at him, trying to make sense of what Sean was saying and why he would be saying it.

"No, he wasn't." The color had drained from his face and as he reached over to take her hand, she pulled it away.

She couldn't move. She couldn't speak.

"As you know, my father—God, rest his soul—was the sheriff in those years…" He paused like he was hoping she would put the pieces together for herself, but how could she? She had no idea what was coming.

He ran his finger down the cold steel of his fork. "Cameron had been the one driving. That part was true. He and I had been partying together that night."

"That's a lie," she countered, sounding breathless. "You two didn't hang out. You weren't even friends."

He looked at her, and she could have almost sworn there were tears in his eyes.

She felt no pity.

"He and I grew up together. We didn't hang out in high school. We were in different crowds, but he lived three houses down." He made a choking sound, as though his feelings were swelling in his throat.

She couldn't even begin to count the number of times she had that pressure, that pain…that tremendous grief.

"There had been that kegger—he didn't want to tell you about it. He knew you'd be upset that he was going, but he told me he wanted to have one last bender before having to really grow up and become a dad. He'd been drinking. *You know.*"

Cameron's dad had told her they had smelled alcohol in the car at the time of the accident, but no one had ever told her *he* had been drinking and driving. Many times, she had wondered, but she'd always come to the conclusion that he was smarter than that…that he'd known what was at stake. More, he'd known she was there waiting for him and needing him to step up and be the man she needed him to be in a moment when she needed someone to help her more than ever.

He'd *promised.*

She'd been so stupid. So naive.

"He was so nervous about becoming a father. It was all he could talk about. Most of the guys actually kind of got tired of hearing about you and the baby. A few had even told him he'd lost his mind…" He paused. "I don't know why I'm telling you about that, but…"

"Just say it. Tell me everything," she said, but her voice was laced with venom, and it burned on her lips.

"He'd come by himself to the kegger. It got late. My friends wanted to stay out there and keep partying, but I'd promised my dad I would go to work the next day. He didn't know where I was…only that I was staying at my friend's house."

She got up and took her plate over to the kitchen sink and set it on the counter. She turned around, crossing her arms over her chest as she fought to control the pain in her heart. Waving, she motioned for him to continue.

"I told Cameron to let me drive. I hadn't been drinking as much as he had been. He was pretty wasted. Neither of us should have ever gotten in that car." A single tear slipped down his cheek. "He hit that tree going at least fifty. I don't remember anything about the accident except waking up and looking for him. There was a hole in the windshield. I had to cut myself out of my seat belt. I went outside. Cameron was still alive."

He looked down at his hands as though he could still see Cameron resting in them. They were as good as still covered in blood.

"I held him… I held him when he took his last breath."

Wordlessly, she walked out of the kitchen and out of Sean's life.

Chapter Eleven

He hadn't thought his revelation would go well, but it had gone a million times worse than he had anticipated. April hated him.

She had every right.

He'd wanted to tell her that he'd tried to save Cameron. That he'd done chest compressions.

More, he wanted to tell her that he'd been carrying the weight of his failures ever since that night.

So many nights, he had wished he had died, if not in place of Cameron, then right beside him. There had been no reason for him to walk away while Cameron hadn't.

Yet, April must have known he'd failed without his ever having to explicitly tell her. If he had succeeded in his life-saving measures, then she wouldn't have been standing with him. She would have had a life somewhere with Cameron and their baby, Ann, and possibly more children, in tow.

He'd cost her a future.

A renewed sense of guilt coursed through him.

He should have been the one to go that day.

He sat down on the couch in the living room and put his head in his hands. Maybe he shouldn't have told her what had happened, or what role he'd played in it. She'd still be here if he'd kept the past in the past, but no. He just had to get his trauma off his chest.

Telling her had been absolutely selfish. That night and its consequences in his life were his to bear.

He should have borne them in silence.

Then again, if she had found out any other way…

He wiped the back of his hand over his face, roughly pushing away the tears that had dampened his cheeks in yet another moment of weakness. Here he had thought he was a strong man, a man capable of saving others and making a difference when he couldn't even do those things in his own life. All he was good at was destruction and death.

Piston rubbed against his leg, pulling him from his self-loathing.

"Hey buddy," he said, reaching down and rubbing the cat's ear. "She's not coming back."

The cat sat down and looked up at him like he could understand what he was trying to tell him.

"I know you're not surprised," he said, answering the question on Piston's furry face.

The cat meowed loudly.

He perched on his elbow. "Don't yell at me. I didn't do it on purpose."

Piston meowed again and ran to the door of the kitchen and looked back at him like he wanted him to follow.

"Yeah, yeah, I'm sure you want some food," he said, getting up and walking after the cat.

It was wrong, but he was glad his furry friend was here to save him from the fiery inferno of his thoughts. Piston pranced down the hall, turning back every few feet before lurching ahead. Instead of leading him to his food bowl, he led him to the back bedroom.

"I told you, she's not coming back," he argued.

Piston meowed loudly again and rushed into the room.

Though he didn't really want to go into the room and stare at the bed, which would inevitably remind him of last night's close call, he followed.

As he walked in, Piston rubbed against the bedside table. Sitting on top was April's cell phone. In her rush to walk out, she must have forgotten it.

"Son of a…" he said, walking over and picking it up.

The screen lit up with a notification that she had missed fourteen calls.

She hadn't been gone that long—maybe thirty minutes. He wondered how many were from her stalker.

Though he wanted to open up the phone and take a look to validate his suspicions, he didn't bother. It was an invasion of her privacy, and he doubted he could have gotten past her security anyway. It was better to just give it back to her, phone undisturbed.

He put the phone in his pocket, knowing full well that she wouldn't be coming back…not even for her device. If he was in her shoes and she had dropped that kind of bomb on him, he would just get a new cell phone before ever giving in and coming back.

In order to save her the thousand bucks, the least he could do was to take her phone over to her apartment and drop it off. He didn't even have to talk to her. He could just knock and hand it off *if* she chose to answer the door.

If she wasn't there or if she refused to see him, he could leave it in her mailbox or something.

Piston rubbed against his leg, like he was looking for acknowledgment of his good deed.

"Yes, buddy, thank you." He reached down and picked up the gray beast.

Walking out, he made his way to the kitchen where he kept everything for Piston. He pulled out a can of wet food and flopped it out into his dish. "You earned it." He let Piston down beside his bowl and he chowed down on the special treat.

Grabbing his keys, he made his way out to his pickup. As he turned toward the driver's-side door, he was surprised to find April standing there, leaning against it. She looked slightly disheveled, but it made sense. He had sprung his information almost as soon as she had gotten out of bed.

I'm such a jerk, he thought.

He didn't have a clue what to do or say to make things better between them. "Have you been here ever since you left?" He felt stupid leading with that, but he hadn't been expecting to see her.

"I started to walk toward my apartment, but I came back." She tucked her hands in tighter to her pits, hugging herself.

"Did you realize you left this behind?" he asked, pulling out her phone. "Piston found it."

She took it and clicked on the screen, giving a long sigh. "Thanks." She turned off the screen and pushed it into her pocket. "That's actually not why I came back, though. In fact, I could probably live without it for reasons that I'm sure you're aware of."

"Then why did you come back? Did you forget something else?"

"We need to find Grace."

So, she only came back because he was the only one who could help her find answers. *Got it.*

He couldn't be mad she was using him, not when they were helping someone else. Yet, he couldn't stop from coming full circle. "Why?"

She frowned like she hadn't understood his question.

"Why are you so fervent that we find Grace? Do you know something about her disappearance that you haven't told me?"

As soon as he spoke, her calm, but guarded facade faded away and was replaced by anger. "You know, you don't always have to say and do the most wrong things."

"Gah," he said, rubbing his face angrily. "I'm sorry. You're right."

"Look, Sean, I'm going to let you just sit with what you've said and done." She sighed. "I don't need to beat you up any more than I'm sure you've already being doing for the last sixteen years."

That didn't mean that she could or would forgive him. In fact, it didn't mean anything more than she was going to let him hang himself with his guilt.

"I want you to know how sorry I am…for *everything*." He reached for her hand, but she stepped back. Her rejection was like a slap in the face. "Please, tell me you forgive me."

"I can't forgive you for what happened." Tears filled her eyes, but she blinked them away. "What happened…it destroyed me in so many ways. It ended so many things. I'd be lying if I said I could forgive you. When it comes to that night, that accident—there isn't a single person involved who wasn't at fault—from the person who told him about the party, to the people who handed him a beer, and then later the ones who watched him get in the car to drive."

Chapter Twelve

April could tell he wanted to keep talking and begging for her forgiveness, but she wasn't ready to hear anything else he had to say. If it weren't for Grace, she wouldn't have come back, wouldn't have set foot within thirty yards of him, but there were immediate needs that were more important than what had happened.

"April, I'm sorrier than you could even know. If there was any way I could go back—"

She stopped him with the wave of her hand. "I don't want to hear any more. I can't. Let's just find our girl, and then you and I—we can go our separate ways."

"But—" He started to argue.

"There are no *buts*. There's only finding Grace. That's all." She paused, trying not to focus on the anger and pain that were moving through her. "If you can't handle it… I can work alone."

Her phone buzzed in her pocket. She didn't want to look in case it was Damon—her stalker. She didn't need to pull the pin on that grenade by answering it; there were already more emotional land mines than she could get through.

It buzzed again, and Sean looked at her expectantly. "At least look. What if it's Grace?"

She pulled her phone out and glanced at it, but was annoyed with herself for doing what she was told when all she really wanted was to tell him that he had ruined her life.

"It's not," she said, recognizing the number as one of Damon's. She shoved it back in her pocket. "Let's just go and check on the fire scene."

He walked toward the passenger's door and opened it, quietly holding it for her.

The ride to the duplex was a silent one. She had focused on her breathing and the anger that kept boiling up in her core, making her want to yell and scream and tell him about the night terrors of car accidents and lost babies that she still experienced.

What if the person I'm mad at is myself?

She pushed the thought down. She was glad she had someone else to blame for what had happened. She couldn't blame Cameron. Every time she tried to point a finger and find a reason he had died, she had always come back to herself—her pregnancy was why he had gone out that night. *She* was the one who had mistakenly gotten pregnant. If *she* hadn't, he wouldn't have gotten so drunk or at least he wouldn't have had to drive. He had been driving to get back to *her.*

Now, it really could be someone else's fault—the pain and self-flagellation, it could all be focused on *Sean. He* had been the last one to see Cam alive.

If *he* had only taken the keys and made Cam stay at that party. The anger within her rose and threatened to spill over as the new information reopened old wounds.

Sean turned left and after a few minutes, he pulled to a stop in front of the still-smoldering structure that had once been Grace's apartment. There was a van marked Fire Marshal parked outside. He turned to her and looked as though he was going to ask her a question, but he shut his mouth and turned off the engine and got out.

He walked around to her side and held out his hand to help her out of the pickup, but she carefully avoided his touch.

"April..." He said her name like it was an apology.

"Let's just worry about her being in that fire. I need to know she's still alive."

He nodded.

"Did anyone ever run a trace on her phone?" she asked.

"The police ran one on the day she went missing from the hospital, but the last time she had turned it on had been at the hospital. As far as them running another, I don't know." He pulled out his phone. "I texted the detective who was helping with Grace's disappearance."

She looked over at the duplex. Since they had left last night, the place had continued to burn. The doors and windows had been smashed in. There was a hole in the roof that was burned through and stained by smoke.

The place was a total loss.

An overweight older man walked toward them with a clipboard in his hand.

"Hey, Jim, how's it going?" Sean asked, meeting the man out on the sidewalk, which led to what had been the front door but was now a jagged, charred hole.

The older gentleman straightened the white uniform shirt he was wearing, leaving behind a black ashy handprint right at the center of his belly. She couldn't stop staring at it, even though she couldn't think why. "Hi, Sean. It's going."

"I tried to call you," Sean said. "Find anything?"

"This and that," he said, glancing over at her like he wasn't sure of what he could or couldn't say in her presence.

"She's helping us with locating Grace," Sean said, having picked up on his fellow firefighter's nonverbal question as well.

"I haven't been on scene very long. Working the perimeter before heading inside. So, no major news about the possible vic, everyone is safe and accounted for and we've been told that Grace's foster parents are out of town and unreachable for a few days, but—" He motioned for them to follow him around to the side of the building. There, where he must have been working when they'd arrived, was a black tactical bag.

As he got near his bag, he gave them a small, triumphant smile. "I believe that whoever started this fire used some sort of accelerant."

"So, you think it was an arson?" April asked.

"Absolutely." Jim nodded. "As for finding who lit the match and then proving that in court, well, that's always the highest hurdle."

"Did you find anything that could indicate who may have started it?" Sean asked.

"Nothing to do with that yet, but look." He pointed at a strange line on the ground. "See that sheen there?" he asked, motioning toward an opalescent circle on the ground near the linear burn mark. "That looks like some kind of petroleum product."

"Is it oil?" April asked. "Wouldn't it take longer to get it going than something, say, like gasoline?"

Jim smirked. "Right?" He squatted and pulled out a swab from his bag. Taking it out of its paper wrapper, he dabbed it near the linear burn mark. He wafted the smell toward himself. "*Ha!* Here, take a whiff. I think we may have our answer. *Maybe.*"

He lifted the swab for her to smell. The swab carried a strong oily smell of burned gasoline.

"They used oil and gas?" she asked, confused.

Jim glanced at Sean like he was trying to see if Sean was following his thinking or not. "Actually," Jim said, "I'm thinking that whoever did this tried to start the fire with diesel fuel first…and realized that wouldn't work well enough to get the fire really going and then decided to use regular gasoline."

"Where did they get the gas?" she asked. "Or diesel, for that matter?"

He glanced around them and toward the neighbor's house. "That's a good question. There are trucks that take diesel, but so do tractors."

No one around appeared to be driving a diesel pickup or have a tractor.

Jim took the swab and placed it in his collection kit. He took a few pics with scales and then stood up. He walked toward the back corner of the house as he continued to take more pictures of the full scene. He stopped moving and snapped another series of pictures. "Ah, hell."

She followed Sean toward him. There, near Jim's foot, was what she recognized as a yellow clip-style cap for the end of a gas can.

Jim moved toward his bag but stopped and turned toward Sean. "As much as I appreciate you guys stopping by, this is starting to look like a crime scene, so…"

"Sorry, man," Sean said, touching her arm. "We'll get out of your hair, but if there's anything you need from us—"

"Or, if you find anything out about the missing girl…" she interrupted.

"Yes, please call us," Sean said, looking at her with a small smile.

Jim nodded. "You got it. I'm hoping she isn't in there, and nothing bad has happened to her."

"We are, too," she said.

"Did you manage to get in touch with the people who were on the lease, Grace's foster parents?" Sean asked.

Jim shook his head. "I'll text you their numbers, but so far, they haven't been picking up. However, on their social media pages it looks like they have been active." He looked over at April. "And don't worry, we're going to do everything in our power to try to locate this girl—one way or another. We need to provide her family with some answers."

The way he said those words brought back thoughts of Cameron. Those were the same words she had heard when she'd gotten the news of his death. She could still hear them ringing in her ears when Cameron's father had come over and told her what had happened. *April, at least we got answers, and we know what happened.*

After Sean's revelation, and more than ever, she knew the truth about answers—they were nothing more than convenient lies.

Chapter Thirteen

It was official. April would never forgive him for what he'd done. Any hopes he'd ever had on making things right were gone—not to mention the thoughts he'd had of holding her on his chest. It was all ruined, and her hatred for him was completely justified.

The best, and only, thing he could do now was get through these days until they found Grace. *Hopefully.* He couldn't think about the possibility that they wouldn't...or that she was inside that burned-out building.

He took another look at the apartment as they pulled away from the curb. If April hadn't been with him, he was sure Jim would have had him help out on the investigation, but he wasn't about to leave her—though, it would have been easier on his head and his heart.

Plus there were other leads they needed to look into.

First things first, he needed to locate Grace's guardians. His phone pinged with a text from Jim, who'd sent him their names and numbers. He called the male and then the female, but neither picked up. He pulled up social media and went to their profiles. There, on the woman's profile, was a picture of her and her husband standing hand in hand in Playa del Carmen, thanks to her pin.

At least they didn't have to worry about them being inside their apartment at the time of the fire—or, that they'd had any obvious role in creating the fire. However, as he scrolled through the woman's page, he found picture after picture of them on vacation—all without children. "Did Grace have any siblings?" he asked. "At least, any that were staying with the same foster parents?"

"I don't think so. Why?"

He moved her phone so she could see the pictures of the vacationing couple. "From this and the time stamps, these two have been in Mexico for more than two months."

"Are you kidding me?" She grabbed the phone out of his hand and started scrolling through the pictures. "No way."

"What?" he asked, not understanding why she would be surprised or upset with the news.

"Grace has only been at Sulphur Springs for a little over six weeks." She dropped his phone on the dashboard, with a huff. "That means her foster parents had left her alone and completely unsupervised until she came and stayed with us." She ran her hands over her face.

"They can't do that, can they?" He didn't know the laws or statutes around what constituted appropriate care of a teenager in the system. From what he had heard and picked up on the job, there were some foster parents who were great and went above and beyond, while there were other guardians who were only participating in order to milk the system.

"No, they can't leave a child alone for a month and go out of the country. Are you kidding me?" she asked, looking at him like he was dumb.

"I didn't mean it like that, just that at what age—"

"Do those who monitor the foster children's welfare stop caring so much?" she said, finishing his question.

"Well…" *Yes.*

She shook her head and started tapping away on her phone. He could see she was texting someone, but he didn't recognize the woman's name.

"Who are you talking to?" he asked.

"I'm texting my friend at child protection services. I think they should be made aware of everything that's going on—though I assume my boss has filled them in already," she said, typing even faster and grabbing screenshots of the guardians' social media posts.

For a moment, he wondered if that's where Grace had gone, but there was no way Grace would have gone to CPS to get help. He had never heard of any child, not even a teenager, who'd reached out to their caseworker. That didn't mean it wasn't possible, but very unlikely given the circumstances.

"Seriously?" April grumbled at her phone.

"Hmm?"

"Grace's caseworker hadn't been notified of anything. She hadn't even been told that Grace was in the hospital." She balled her hand into a fist. "My boss must have assumed the hospital informed them, and vice versa." She sighed. "It's just no wonder that these kids fall between the cracks. Between systematic failures, foster care neglect and the accident, well, it's no damned wonder Grace was having social problems. She's never had a chance."

He hadn't known Grace for very long, but he could say with every certainty that the world had failed her. *He* had failed her, too. He should have checked in on her at the hospital more often.

He'd become a firefighter and SAR team member to

help others, and when presented with his chance, he had fallen short...again.

"What did the caseworker say?" he asked.

She shrugged. "That she was glad of the notification. She was sorry to hear what had happened, and they would put feelers out as to Grace's whereabouts."

"But basically, they're as limited in resources as we are."

She pointed at him. "*That*. Exactly. Plus each of these caseworkers is assigned dozens of cases. They can only sacrifice so much time. And the lady made a point of Grace having a great deal of social issues. She, too, thinks Grace is nothing more than a runaway."

This poor girl was being abandoned at every turn. Except, by them.

Yet, he doubted Grace would guess they were out there searching for her.

The girl was vulnerable in many ways—unstable home, no money, she hadn't even turned to her friends. If she hadn't simply run away like everyone assumed, she would be a prime target for a predator.

Regardless of how she had gone missing, she was going to be facing a variety of possible horrors—from human trafficking to falling in with the drug culture. That was, if she was still alive after the fire.

He shook off the thought. She had to be alive. They just had to locate her.

He started to drive around the small town, slowing down as they made their way past the local movie theater, then they worked through the tiny downtown and finally drove through the residential area full of tiny houses and toward Summer's duplex.

There were resources the local law enforcement officers

could tap into, but as a firefighter and even a SAR worker, some of his reach was limited. If he could have, though, he would have loved to do another ping on her cell phone.

At the thought of phones, April's buzzed on the dashboard. She reached for it and glanced at the caller's information. She tapped on the screen and answered, putting it on speaker. "Hello?"

He could hear a woman crying and then a strange muffled, shuffling sound. There was a deeper sound, like that of a man's voice, but he couldn't make out any words.

"Grace? Is that you?" April's voice was high and frantic. "Grace, are you okay? Where are you?"

The line went dead.

"Oh, my God," she said, covering her mouth with her hand as she looked over at him. "Do you think…? That couldn't have been her, right? But if it was her…she's alive."

At least, for now, he thought, not daring to speak those words aloud.

"Who was on the caller ID?" he asked.

She tapped on her phone, pulling up the information. "There wasn't a name. It was just a location. It says the number was out of Gillette, Wyoming."

He knew the town well. It was a coal mining town with a railroad that ran through its heart. Despite the rolling hills and antelope, Gillette wasn't a place he would ever have wanted to call home.

That being said, it was within the area Grace could have traveled in the time since she had been missing. Or, it could have just been a random number used by an app and it had nothing to do with the caller's actual location. "Call the number back."

It would surprise most people, but thanks to Gillette's location along the interstate and its access to a main railroad line, the town was prime country for human traffickers. From what he'd heard on the street, it was a regular thing for the Wyoming cops to bust drug runners hoping to get to Chicago and other big cities.

She called the number back, but it went straight to a generic voicemail.

"Damn it!" she yelled, slamming her hand against the dashboard.

"It's okay. Don't get too upset. Maybe it wasn't even her."

She glared at him. "It was her. I know it was Grace. You *know* it was her, too."

He had to hope it wasn't. That the crying wasn't coming from the girl they were looking for, but it was all too coincidental for it not to be. In his entire life, he couldn't think of a time when he'd gotten a random call with a woman crying on the other end of the line, and then the line going dead. The odds of it being anyone else besides Grace were astronomical.

"Sean, she's in trouble. She needs help. She needs us." She looked back down at her phone, calling the number again, but it went to voicemail. "There has to be something we can do."

He turned the truck around and hit the gas, going as fast they could safely go. He screeched to a halt in front of the sheriff's office.

She kept dialing Grace's phone, but no one answered.

The thing must have been shut off.

"Let's go," he said, turning off his truck. "These guys are our best bet if she calls back."

She nodded, but didn't look up from her phone, almost as if she thought that at any second, it would ring again, and Grace would be there.

He rushed around to her side of the truck and helped her out, but she still refused to look away from the little screen. She was typing away, sending a text to the number. From what he could see over her shoulder, it looked like she'd already sent several others.

They rushed into the main lobby of the sheriff's office, where a secretary was talking on the phone. She spotted them and motioned for them to take a seat in the hard blue plastic chairs that were in front of her desk.

Yeah, he wasn't playing that game. Instead, Sean stood at the edge of the desk. "Ma'am, I'm sorry to interrupt, but we need to talk to the officer in charge of walk-ins today."

The woman frowned at him, silently admonishing him for his rudeness, but he didn't care.

"It's important that we see him, *now.*"

She put her hand over the mouthpiece of her phone. "If it is an emergency, you need to call 911."

He wanted to take the phone she held in her hands and slam it down on the receiver, but instead he forced himself to smile. "We're here about the missing kid. We just got a phone call from her. We need to speak to someone, now… in case she calls back, we need to be prepared."

The woman's mouth moved into an O-shape. "Can you please hold?" she asked the caller. She tapped a button on her phone, and she asked for Detective Terrell.

In less than a minute, Terrell came rolling out. He met them with a smile and a friendly wave. "How's it going, Sean. I hear you've been busy this week."

Sean nodded. "My hands have been full." If he hadn't been so emotionally connected to this case and Grace, he would have joked around with Terrell. They'd known each other ever since he'd gotten started at the fire department, though they didn't often work together.

Terrell's gaze moved to April and the cast on her arm.

"This is my friend April Twofeather. She was the hiker who was hurt in the rockslide the other day. She and I are working to help find Grace Bunchen."

"Nice to meet you, April," Terrell said, with an acknowledging nod and a warm smile. "I'm glad to see you're up and running."

"Thanks," she said tersely, but her body was almost so tense that she was nearly vibrating.

"So, I hear you may have been in contact with Grace?"

April nodded.

"Why don't you guys follow me into my office and fill me in on the details." He motioned for them to follow as he used his key card to open a large steel door that led to the inner sanctum of the department.

As they walked, April talked fast about the phone call. Terrell simply nodded as they walked down the industrial-carpeted hallway and to his office, which was at the end of the corridor. There were three other officers working on computers as they walked by, which meant they were about as fully staffed as they could be at any given time during the day. Currently, there were only about ten deputies working for the vast, low-population county.

Terrell stopped and closed the door as they walked in and sat down in the proffered chairs. "So, and please bear with me here, I'm not trying to be insensitive," Terrell started, as he walked to the other side of his desk and sat down in the quiet office, "but what you're telling me is that you don't have definitive proof that this phone call was from Grace, but merely a heavy suspicion?"

When he said it like that, Sean felt foolish for bulling his way into the department and Terrell's office.

"I *know* it was her," April pressed. "I don't give my number out very often. No one else I know is currently in trouble."

"Wait…" Terrell put his hands up. "April, if I recall, you work for Sulphur Springs. Yes?"

She nodded.

"So, you're telling me that you don't get calls from other girls who need you from time to time? And again, I am really not trying to be an ass, I just want to get my bearings here. That's all."

April answered with an annoyed huff. "Look, I do *on occasion* hear from other kids who need my help, but I know with every fiber of my being that this call came from Grace."

Terrell nodded and glanced over at Sean. The detective's button-down shirt was pulled tight over his bulletproof vest as though the guy had gained some weight since he'd bought the thing.

Sean had always liked Terrell, but he could understand April's annoyance. "I heard the call as well. And, Detective Terrell, I can understand your trepidation in looking into this. But here's how I see it," he said, leaning onto the edge of the desk and tenting his fingers in the detective's direction, "if this was Grace calling, then we have a great lead. If it is some other girl who needs our help, then great…we can help her, too. Either way, we have a girl out there who needs to be rescued."

Terrell nodded and turned toward his computer. "Can you tell me the number? I'll see what we can do."

April read off the Gillette, Wyoming, number, Terrell

tapping it into the computer. He moved closer to the screen and sat his chin in his hand as he scrolled through whatever results he was poring over.

"Anything?" Sean asked after a long moment.

Terrell looked back at him. "So, the number comes back to a company with an LLC registered out of Gillette. Something called Mango Tango. You guys ever heard of it?"

"No," April said as Sean shook his head.

Terrell hit a few more buttons and, as he worked, his features darkened.

"What's going on?" Sean asked.

Terrell looked over at them like he had almost forgotten they were there. He stood up. "I appreciate you guys letting me know about the call. I'll see what we can do on our end."

The detective walked around the side of his desk and motioned for them to get up and follow him out. It was awkward and forced, and it made Sean wonder what exactly he didn't want to tell them about what he was finding. Regardless, he didn't like the way Terrell was acting.

"Wait… That's it?" April asked. "You're kicking us out? You're not going to tell us what you found? Was it Grace who called?"

Terrell glanced back at his computer. "Look, I can't tell you much, but I can tell you that company is tied in with some pretty shady dealings. Lots of criminals use their tech to cover their tracks."

"So, Grace is in the hands of a criminal…" April reached over to Sean with her uninjured arm as though she needed his help to remain standing.

Sean held her hand but put his other arm around her back to help support her. "Do you need April's phone or anything—in case she calls back, or to trace the number or whatever?"

Terrell shook his head. "Just make sure that you guys let me know if you hear anything." He looked to April. "Rest assured, April, I will do my best to see if we can locate our victim."

Chapter Fourteen

April didn't care if they had to walk all the way to Wyoming to check every phone, but they would be doing something to get their hands on Grace. From the look on the detective's face, every minute that she was missing counted.

She rushed out of the sheriff's office and got into Sean's truck. He was ten steps behind, and his lack of speed irritated her. Didn't he realize what was at stake?

As she clicked her seat belt and waited, she reminded herself how invested he was in this…at least, he seemed to be. Yet, now that she knew the truth behind his motivations—that he felt guilty—she didn't feel the same as she had before.

It was crazy to think that he had played a role in Cameron's death as a kid, but as an adult, he had *saved her*. Now he was trying to save someone else. If anything, he'd saved many people.

If she accepted life for what it had wrought, and the man who'd played such a pivotal role in hers, she wasn't sure what the future would bring, and she wasn't sure she was ready to find out.

However, she would be lying to herself if she tried to refute the fact that it had been her first instinct to seek out his touch when she'd needed support in the office. Her body and her mind were at odds.

As he got into the truck, he was tapping away on his phone. She was grateful he'd gotten in and she could go back to their immediate needs instead of spiraling down the depths of her soul. Perhaps keeping things surface level with Sean was the best for everyone involved—which meant leaving the past in the past.

For now, that would be best.

"We driving to Gillette?" she asked.

"You and I both know that she could be just about anywhere. Just because a phone is registered in one state, it doesn't mean it's there."

Of course, he was right, but that didn't make her want to go there any less. "I don't care. It's our first real, verified information."

"And I'm sure Terrell will run with it. We don't have the resources he does. We have to trust that he will do his job."

Again, she couldn't argue with his logic. "Then what do you think we should do? We have to do something."

He scowled. "Terrell texted me as soon as we left."

"And?"

"He said that he thinks he has a name of a guy who is associated with the LLC. He is looking into it."

There was a slight sense of relief. The detective was working fast and had not simply been patronizing them. Finally, it felt like they were starting to get somewhere.

"What about the fire?" she asked.

"I'm hoping the phone call proves that Grace wasn't killed, but we are making some major assumptions. Again, that call could have been anyone." He started the pickup and glanced over at her like she knew something he didn't. "What are you thinking about the fire?"

"It's just weird that Grace's duplex burns down and now this…"

He tapped on his steering wheel as he backed out of the parking spot. "Just because strange things have been happening doesn't mean that everything is related. I mean… do you think someone caused the rockslide you were involved with?"

His words felt like a fist in the gut. She wasn't sure if he had meant to hurt her, but it didn't matter…here he was, once again bringing up the sore spots in her life. "No," she said, shaking her head, "I don't think anyone caused that slide…at least no one other than me."

He quirked a brow. "Why do you think you caused it?"

She paused, thinking about the moments before the slide and her begging Grace to come her way. "I shouldn't have had those kids on the mountain that day, not after all that heavy rain. I should have known the conditions were too questionable." As she spoke, her admission reminded her of his admission to her…how if only he hadn't let Cameron drive.

He looked pained, like his thoughts had gone there, too.

She wanted to address it, but instead she clamped her mouth shut.

Silence and pain filled the space between them in the truck. Until finally, she couldn't stand it anymore. "Can you please take me home?"

"If that's what you want." He nodded, but his face had turned hard. "But what about looking for Grace?"

She had no intention of stopping her search, but she couldn't stand being in this weird limbo with him any longer. She needed a reprieve and time to come to terms with everything that had happened over the course of the last few days.

"What about Wyoming?" he continued.

"Wyoming isn't the answer. We would just be chasing our tails," she said, a sickening lump in her throat. It was hard to believe how defeated she suddenly felt. "Besides, for all we know, that really wasn't her on that phone call. What if I was wrong?"

"Why are you second-guessing yourself all of a sudden, April?" He looked over at her, searching her face. "I didn't mean to make you feel bad, or to make everything that has happened somehow your fault."

"No, but you made me realize how her disappearance is all my doing. For once, Grace had been cared for and safe—while she was at Sulphur Springs. That was, until I made a stupid decision and failed her so much that it nearly cost her life." Tears threatened to creep up into her eyes.

She blinked hard, trying to keep her emotions and their tells at bay.

"I will absolutely do as you wish. I'm not going to make you stay and work with me if you're not comfortable or if I've done something to upset you, but I have to say that I think we work better as a team. You know her better than I do, but I have more resources and connections." He reached over and put his hand, palm up, on the console between them like he wanted her to touch him once again.

She wanted to. Oh, she wanted to. Yet, if she did, it would mean more than just their holding hands. It would mean that she was going to try to forgive him and the hell he'd wrought on her life. She didn't know if she was ready. Everything was happening so fast between and around them.

Her phone buzzed in her pocket, and it pulled her away

from her whirlpool of thoughts, thoughts that all came back to Grace. She took out her phone and glanced at the name—Damon.

She let out a long, exasperated sigh. Of course, it would be him. He hadn't called thirty times already today; he was behind. She ignored the call.

"Is it him?"

"Damon? Yes." She nodded.

He pulled his hand back and put it on his knee. She tried not to pay attention to the little niggle of disappointment that moved up from her core.

"At least this time he is calling from his original number. He must really want me to know that *he* is still calling."

"Let's get you a new number today—"

"That's out of the question. If Grace tries to call again…" She waved him off. Putting up with being harassed by some idiot so she didn't miss a chance with Grace was worth it.

"Are you sure this guy isn't dangerous? Do you know if he owns or has access to any weapons?"

"It's Montana, everyone has access to, or owns, guns, but I don't think he wants me dead. I think he just wants me to agree to be his girlfriend. The guy is cracked, but if he wasn't, I would have to say I was almost flattered by his persistence."

Sean shook his head at her admission.

She had said too much. Of course, he wouldn't understand why she felt as she did. Logically, she was more than aware that Damon wasn't acting like a normal or rational man, but at the same time, she'd been in relationships in which the guy couldn't even find time to text her back— at a certain level, it felt good to be wanted, even if it was by the wrong person.

Maybe, the right person is the one sitting next to me. She shoved the thought away.

What would it say about her as a person if she fell for Sean and forgave him for throwing her life off the path so dramatically?

He was the reason she'd been forced to give up her child.

But was it really fair to put the burden of that decision on him?

She groaned as the phone in her hand buzzed to life again. *Damon.*

"Do you want me to talk to him again?"

She didn't know what she wanted, or how to feel. She didn't want to be dealing with this at all, and especially not when there were greater worries in her life. So, she handed off her phone. "Knock yourself out. Maybe you can get the message to him better than I've been able to."

He pulled the truck to the side of the road and answered the phone on speaker.

"April?" Damon's voice bounced around the inside of the truck like a thrown grenade.

She opened her mouth to answer, but Sean shook his head. "This isn't April, Damon."

"Oh, so it's you again? Her little rescuer?" Damon answered with a mirth-filled laugh. "She's got you all whipped, doesn't she?"

"This is my phone now, Damon. If you keep trying to get in contact with April, I'm going to help her to file a restraining order against you."

Damon's laugh was louder this time. "Do whatever the hell you want to do. She is still going to come back to me. She may fool around with you, but I'm the man she really wants."

"No, I don't, Damon," April said. "I never wanted you." She couldn't help herself. She had to speak up.

Sean's eyes darkened and he shook his head and mouthed *no*.

Though she didn't want to, she had to say something. This was her fault and her stalker; it was her responsibility to take care of. She shouldn't have handed off her phone.

She stuck out her hand and motioned for the device, but Sean shook his head.

Damon went quiet, then, "April?"

"Yes, Damon, it's me."

Sean tilted his head back against the headrest in annoyance, but then glanced down at the phone.

"April, is he making you act this way?" Damon asked. "We both know you love me."

"No, Damon, I don't. I told you, I'm not interested." A thrill moved through her as she found pride in her resolve to say "no" to this man with Sean watching. "I don't want you, and I don't want you to contact me anymore."

"This doesn't sound like you, April."

"It is her," Sean growled. "She made her feelings clear. Now, leave her alone."

"I want to hear that from her mouth," Damon countered.

"You just did," she said, not missing a beat. "Leave me alone, Damon."

It felt so good to make a stand against him. Though she had tried before, something about this time, about the level of resolve in her voice and the stiffness in her spine…he would listen. He had to know she was serious.

The phone went dead, and Sean handed it back to her.

"I'm sorry—" she started, but the look on Sean's face made her go quiet.

"April, you have nothing to feel sorry about." He sighed. "I'm sorry I tried to silence you. I don't know why, but it feels like I'm never doing the right thing when it comes to you—no matter how hard I try."

She could understand why he felt that way. "I know how you feel, Sean. I felt like I made a huge mistake right there, interceding when you were trying to protect me. *Again*." The word drifted in the air like a feather.

"You're welcome." He reached over and pushed a strand of hair off her face.

The soft touch of his fingers on her skin made her heart race. She loved the way he touched her, like she needed care, but also with respect.

"I just wish I knew what I could do to make him go away."

"For now, let's just go radio silence. No more contact until we can work something out with your phone." She reached up and touched the hand that was still lingering at the edge of her ear.

"I hope you know that I do appreciate your help with this," she said, clasping his fingers. She wasn't sure if she wanted to talk about the rest of her feelings having to do with Cameron, but she knew she needed to at least say something so he didn't make the wrong assumptions about how she was thinking. "As for what happened in high school…" She paused as she searched for the right words. "I need some more time to make sense of my feelings. I'm sure you can understand that there's no manual on how to feel in a situation like ours."

He cocked his head to the side slightly, his eyes catching the light, and it made the blue of them more vibrant than she would have ever thought possible. "How would you explain a situation like ours?"

She chewed at her lip. *Right man, wrong time. Wrong man, right time*, she thought. *And no matter what I think, what would Cameron say?*

"You saved my life. I'm eternally grateful—"

"But?"

She wasn't going to say *but*. In fact, she didn't really know how she was going to finish her sentence. "All I know is that I'm more attracted to you than I think I *should* be."

A smile lit up his features as he gave her hand a gentle squeeze. "It ain't much, but for now, that's enough."

Chapter Fifteen

He hated this Damon guy. He hated him with every fiber of his being. Had it not been for the situation with Grace, he would have been on the guy's porch and ready for a fight.

It took everything in his power not to tell her that how she felt about the situation was wholly and unequivocally wrong. What was happening to her wasn't her fault. Her responding like a normal, kind and polite adult wasn't why this guy had decided to be an unshakable jerk. It was just people like Damon who loved to prey on those who had good souls. He was a predator, pure and simple.

More, the guy had problems. He didn't respect boundaries, and he sure as hell didn't take sound, albeit crass, advice.

Damon would have to eventually listen, though. Sean would make sure of that, one way or another.

He pulled the pickup back onto the road. "Do you still want me to take you home? You know I will, if that is what you really want."

I'm not like Damon. He wanted to say, complete with: *You're safe with me.* But he stayed quiet. He didn't want to talk about Damon with her. In fact, for her sake, he wanted to pretend the guy didn't even exist.

"No matter what, we can't stop searching for Grace," she said, sending him a meaningful and heart-wrenching look.

In so many ways, it felt like they were beating a dead horse. The only bright spot in this was that he was pretty sure April was correct in thinking the phone call had come from Grace.

With that likely assumption, there were few remaining doubts about Grace running away or being taken. It was definitely the latter. However, they had numerous other issues to worry about, and each fear was darker than the last.

Yet, there was still hope Grace was alive.

He was glad Terrell had jumped into action.

His only surprise was that it had taken a damned mysterious phone call from the girl before the police had considered her disappearance legitimate. He could understand being woefully understaffed; it was the nature of the beast when a person worked in a county that was bigger than most states and far less populated, but it always tore at him when minutes mattered.

From the fire standpoint, ten guys ran the station, five on at all points in the day covering an enormous county. Normally, it was more than enough, until the fall fire season hit, and they were inundated with calls from those who lived in remote rural areas; then, it was nonstop calls and no sleep for anyone involved in the firefighting efforts.

"Have you talked to anyone back at the Springs?" he asked.

She shrugged. "The other counselors there haven't said anything."

"What if we run out there? Maybe we can find someone Grace had talked to before the accident."

She nodded. "It's worth a shot, but it's a drive."

He didn't care. He was with the person he wanted to be with. "I think I can suffer through," he said, sending her a playful grin. "I mean, if you can."

She returned his smile. "Being with you is not what I consider suffering..." Her smile widened. "That is, unless you listen to opera or something."

He clicked on an opera channel via Bluetooth. He had no idea what the song was about or who was singing it, but he laughed as April rolled down the window and stuck her head out.

It was so good to finally see her being comfortable with him and joking around. He wasn't sure that they would ever get to this place together again, and he wasn't going to dissect it, but he was relieved. This moment, this time and laughter, was what they both needed.

She pulled her head back in as he turned the volume down. "I take back my suffering comment..." she teased.

His heart lightened in his chest as her eyes sparkled. She really was a beautiful woman. Moving forward, if he got the chance, he would give just about anything to stare into them while he slipped inside of her.

He could almost feel it now, her warmth against him. Kissing her skin. Hell, he'd be happy just to have a chance to hold her in his arms.

"What are you thinking about?"

He jerked. "I..." He couldn't tell her the truth. Things were finally starting to go well with her, and if anything, he was a little embarrassed that he'd been fantasizing about her. "I was just thinking about how much I want to go sky-diving." He smirked.

She cuffed him on the shoulder, the action so teenage-like that it made his pulse race.

He really did have feelings for this woman. Even if she would and could never truly be his, due to the nature of their past, he was grateful for this shared moment in the midst of their continuing drama.

He turned up the radio, singing along like he knew the words. The time flew by as they made their way onto the highway and the thirty minutes out of town. Too soon, she was motioning for him to turn.

If they hadn't been on a mission, he would have kept driving and enjoying their time together.

"Turn at the main entrance," she said.

There was a large, log sign hanging over the entrance to a gravel road that led up into a timbered ravine. The sign read: Welcome to Sulphur Springs, in bold black scrolling. There were bears carved into the left and right sides around the lettering, and the effect was beautiful.

"Is this place only for at-risk youth?" he asked, realizing that for as many times as he had driven by this place on his way out of Big Sky, he'd really never paused to give it much thought.

She nodded. "And their families. We do a lot of work with foster kids."

He turned down the dirt road, driving slowly.

"Sometimes we have group therapy weekends where parents or guardians of our kids can come in and discuss the issues they're facing. Some sessions are with the kids, some without. The owners have tried to develop a location in which everyone can feel safe and secure while also promoting healing and lasting relationships."

It sounded like he needed to spend some time here as well. It had been a long time since he'd been in a lasting relationship. And, as for the healing, he had a feeling that when it came to April—that was a journey in which they could embark upon together.

A large, three-story house came into view at the end of the long, meandering driveway. To its left was a red barn, complete with many horse stalls that led out into a paddock. The entire ranch must have been at least a hundred acres, if not more. It made him wonder who owned the facility and how it had come about.

"There is a steady flow of kids in and out. Sulphur Springs normally houses around fifteen kids, and there are two adult staff members always on duty. Sometimes we have more adults around if there are big events or if parents are here with kids."

"Is it just a camp?" he asked.

"During the school year, we host kids who need temporary housing, and we even have a couple of full-time residents—Andrew and Josie. They are great kids, but because of their ages, have had a hard time getting adopted."

"So, it's a group home?" he asked, pulling to a stop in the parking lot near the front doors.

"It is whatever the kids in this community need." She smiled proudly.

The white house had black shutters, and up close it gave off an air of a place he would have expected in the Deep South, thanks to its Grecian columns and wraparound porch. It was a beautiful, almost palatial house that put the double-wide trailer he'd grown up in to shame.

A boy came out of the front doors and waved as they stepped out of the truck.

"Andrew," April said, joy making her voice high. "How're you doing? You okay?"

The teenager nodded. "Just fine. I'm sorry about your

arm," he said, motioning toward her cast. "How long do you have to wear that thing?"

"They are saying six to eight weeks. It's already feeling like forever, though," she said, stopping beside him and resting her hand on his shoulder.

"I bet. I had a cast when I broke my arm when I was seven. I just remember how badly it itched." The teenager looked over at him. "Who're you?"

"This is Sean McCormack. He was the SAR member who found Grace and me after the slide," April said, scratching at the edge of her cast arm. "Sean saved my life."

The kid nodded appreciatively. "Well done, sir." He stuck out his hand.

"I was just doing my job," Sean said, giving his proffered hand a shake. "I heard what happened up there. If anything, Andrew, it sounds like you are the one who saved everyone. Thanks for getting the other kids to safety and making the call to 911. Without your quick thinking and action, my team wouldn't have stood a chance to reach April and Grace in time. You're the real hero."

Andrew looked at his shoes, embarrassed. "I was just doing what April told me."

She patted his shoulder. "You did a great job. Thank you for saving my life. And…I'm sorry that I put you and the rest of the group in danger."

Sean ached, as he sympathized with her and what she had to have been feeling.

"Everyone's fine." Andrew pointed toward the door. "Well…everyone but Grace. Did you guys find her yet?"

The kid's question slammed into him. "Not yet, but that's why we're here. We were hoping to take some time and talk to everyone." He walked up onto the veranda and leaned against one of the columns. "Do you mind if I ask you a few questions?"

Andrew shrugged and April's hand slipped from him. He made his way over to a porch swing and plopped down as though he was readying himself for an interrogation. "What's up?"

"Do you know if Grace was dating anyone here at the Springs?"

Andrew rubbed at the back of his neck and looked toward the front door, almost as if he was afraid someone was listening from behind it. Or maybe Sean was just connecting dots that weren't really there.

The kid shrugged as he stared at him like he had somehow just given away the fact that he was old and unhip. "I don't know if she was *dating* anyone. That wasn't really her *thing*. She liked to keep things casual. You know… without labels."

Sean nodded. "Did she and anyone here *keep things casual*…you know, hang out or whatever?" He tried to sound cool and relaxed, but he couldn't help his overwhelming feelings of lameness in the face of teenage judgment.

Andrew shrugged noncommittally, but he couldn't meet his gaze.

He really had no idea how April could handle being around these kids every day. While Andrew seemed relatively nice, he could clearly still be a handful. It had to have been hard for April when it came to dealing with the snark and emotional minefields that came with the world of teens.

April stepped closer to the kid on the swing. "Andrew," April said, "it would really be helpful if you could tell me if you know anything about Grace and her private life… We have reason to believe she is in real trouble. She needs help, and we have no idea where we can find her. I know you guys were friends."

Andrew picked at the edge of his fingernail. "We *were* friends."

"What does that mean?" Sean asked.

The kid looked at him like he was speaking out of turn and interfering. He shut his mouth, hoping Andrew would continue to talk.

"It means that she and I had been hooking up here and there. She told me I was one of the reasons she wanted to come to the camp...you know, so we could spend more time together." He put his finger in his mouth and started to chew on his nail for a second. His gaze kept slipping to the door. "We were doing pretty good. You know, getting along. We had even started to talk about what we were gonna do when we got sprung from this place. I'm turning eighteen in like three months, ya know?" He looked at April who nodded. "But you know how things can get."

"What are you thinking about doing, Andrew?" she asked, her voice soft and caring.

"Well, I do pretty good at school, but I'm not getting any scholarships or nothing. So, I figured my best choice was to go to the marines. I've been talking to a recruiter. He's supercool and the jobs sound fun as hell. Plus I could get away from here and see the real world."

He didn't want to tell the kid that no matter where he went in the world, the problems he would face would probably stay the same and life would continue to be a struggle. The only thing that really changed was a person's location.

"You said *was* go to the marines. You still thinking about going in that direction?" April pressed.

Andrew shrugged. "The best part of joining the marines

is that by the time I'd be done with school and stuff, she'd be eighteen. It's only like eighteen months away. We were talking about getting married."

"Married?" Sean choked on the word, surprised. As soon as he spoke, though, he had wished he'd stayed quiet.

"Yeah, you know...the thing where me and my guys have a big party with strippers and all the beer and the next day the chick walks down the aisle in the big dress? That thing."

"Ah. Got it," he said, once again holding back the urge to tell him that life was about to bear down on him and show him how things really went—especially when it came to marriage, and, well, *any* romantic relationship for that matter.

"Last month, though, everything changed. I don't know what happened." He pulled out his phone and started to poke at the screen like it could help him answer the questions surrounding him.

"What changed?" April asked, glancing over at Sean as though telling him that he needed to stay quiet and not interfere.

She could run with this line of questioning all she wanted as long as they got to the bottom of everything. Besides, it was getting clearer by the second that she really was the better one when it came to relating with these kids.

"I don't know what happened. Things were good when she got to camp, but then about a week in everything went downhill," Andrew said, staring at his phone. "She was just all-in one minute and then ghosting me the next. I kept trying to talk to her and figure out what I'd done wrong, but any time I tried she would disappear."

"Did she lose interest once you guys spent more time

together?" Sean asked, knowing this time that he would definitely upset the kid, but not caring. He was tired of trying to work around mercurial adolescent feelings. He just wanted answers.

"Dude," Andrew said, glaring at him.

"All Sean meant was that he wondered if you guys had a falling out...or maybe you guys weren't clicking like you'd hoped? You know?" April said, translating.

"Dude, it wasn't like we weren't together before," Andrew countered. "She and I would talk every day. When her parents were gone, I'd be at her house as much as I could."

"Nights, too?" April asked.

Andrew cringed. "You know we can't break curfew at the Springs."

"That's not what I asked." April sat down beside Andrew and leaned so she could look the kid in his downcast eyes. "I'm not upset, and I'm not going to turn you in for any breach of curfew, but I do need to know what was happening."

"What does it matter if I snuck out at night or not?" He looked away from her. "All that matters is that Grace and I were a thing and now, we aren't."

The front door to the house opened and a shorter than average, dark-haired guy came walking out. He had a sharp chin, the kind that could take a punch, and a scar across his cheek like he'd tested it. He was wearing a red Henley shirt with the arms pushed up with a towel slapped over his shoulder. Though Sean couldn't his finger on the reason why, he already hated the guy.

"Damon," April said, sounding breathless. "What are you doing here?"

"I'm working—you know, like you *should* be." He closed

the door behind himself and walked toward her. He didn't even look in Sean's direction.

Andrew seemed angry as he glanced over at the guy, and it made Sean wonder who hated the guy worse—him or the kid.

Damon turned his back to him. "Things have been hard without you around. How are you feeling? Your arm okay?"

She scowled. "My arm is fine. I'm fine."

"Thanks to your little watchdog, you haven't been answering my calls, but if you had, you'd know that I was trying to check on you. It hurts me when you're hurting. I care about you, April."

April looked down at the ground.

The man's words made chills run down Sean's spine.

"Why don't you just go back inside, Damon?" Sean said, moving between him and April and obstructing Damon's view of his prey. "She doesn't want you out here."

"That's what I bet she told you. That's her little game. Did she also tell you that?" Damon countered, shifting so he could try to look over Sean's shoulder at her, but Sean moved to keep him from glowering at her in an attempt to continue to intimidate.

"Andrew," April said, sounding metered and cautious as she looked at the teenager, "why don't you head back inside. We have some more questions for you, but I'll come see you another time. Okay?"

Andrew stood up from the swing and straightened his pants, pushing his shoulders back and making himself look bigger and more muscular than the little man who'd come out from the house.

Andrew started to walk toward the front door. He glared at Damon. And just like that, Sean liked the kid a little bit more.

"Damon," Andrew said, moving closer to the man.

"Andrew, just shut up and take your ass inside if you know what is good for you. If you don't, I'm going to write you up for insubordination. If I do, you're out on your ass."

"What do I care?" Andrew spit.

"Damon, knock it off," April said, moving beside Andrew and taking him by the arm. "Just because you're having a problem with me doesn't mean you have to take it out on the kids."

It was strange, but Sean felt as though he had walked into some pseudo-world where April and Damon were the parents of the boy and the rest of the kids inside. Maybe it was the fact that they were in authority roles, or maybe it was the fact that April seemed to genuinely care about them, but something about the situation felt *off*. The air between them, April, Andrew and Damon, wasn't exactly what he had expected, and it had thrown him off balance.

What was he missing between them?

What hadn't she told him?

Though April had her hand on Andrew's shoulder, the kid stopped within a step of Damon, and he looked at the man. Before Sean had time to register what was even happening, Andrew had his fist planted square in the center of Damon's gut. Then Andrew grabbed the back of Damon's head and smashed the guy's face against his knee with a sickening crunch.

Damon dropped to the ground, blood pouring from his nose. Andrew moved to jump on top of the man, but April's scream pierced the air and seemed to pull the kid out of his blood-fueled rage.

He spewed expletives, calling Damon every name in

the urban dictionary and several that he wasn't sure he himself understood.

"Andrew! Stop!" April yelled, pulling the kid off Damon.

"I'm sorry, but we both know he has this coming," Andrew said.

"Andrew, enough!" April shouted.

Sean stepped toward the kid and pushed him back. Damon might have gotten what he deserved, however, Andrew didn't need to find himself trouble—Damon was the kind of guy who would press charges. If he did, any chances Andrew had of joining the military would be gone.

Andrew's eyes widened as he looked down at the blood that was oozing out of Damon's nose His mouth opened, and he looked up at April and then at the truck in the parking lot. "I...I'm sorry if you get in trouble. I'm sorry." Andrew grabbed the railing and jumped over the top.

"Just go," April said, almost in a whisper.

He landed on the grass in front of the porch with a thump and he tore off toward Sean's truck. Sean reached down to his pocket. The truck's keys. They were still in the ignition.

Andrew didn't miss a beat as he climbed in and started the pickup. In his wake, he left them standing in a world of dust and blood.

Chapter Sixteen

April couldn't believe what had happened. Andrew was such a good kid, and he had been making the best he could of his life. She'd been proud of him for his choices, all except his last. She knew the kids at the Springs didn't like Damon, but there wasn't a long list of the adults that they did connect with—and even those people weren't unanimously liked.

She was among those who were tolerated and mostly liked, but Grace had proven that even those relationships came with some stiff rules and murky boundaries.

Damon was sitting up against the column, pressing a paper towel to his nose. He looked put out and angry, but she couldn't say that she really cared.

"Call the police," Damon growled. "I want to press charges. He needs to pay."

She shook her head. "Absolutely not. I don't know what you did to that kid, or why he was pissed off with you, but I can almost guarantee you had that coming. You are not going to get him in trouble because someone finally had the strength to stand up to you."

Sean smiled over at her. "If anyone needs to press charges against anyone, it is April against you."

"How dare you threaten me?" Damon countered, dabbing at his nose. There was a cut across the bridge, and it angled slightly to the left.

"Oh, please," April said. "Now, do you want to tell us what you did to upset him so much, or do I need to go inside and start asking the other kids what the hell has been going on?" April asked, motioning toward the house, where she could see a handful of kids pressed against the windows and watching them.

She gave them all a little wave, hoping they would know that regardless of the state of Damon, they had nothing to worry about.

The front door creaked open, and a boy started to walk out.

Sean stepped toward him, blocking him from Damon. "Why don't you go back inside, kiddo?"

The boy, Josh, looked at her questioningly, as though he wasn't sure whether or not to follow the stranger's instructions. April gave him a stiff nod. "Yes. And when you go in, would you please let everyone know that everything's okay? There's no need for concern. In fact, if everyone could please go to the living room and wait, I will come talk to you all in a second."

Sean smiled in approval.

"Are you sure, Ms. Twofeather?" Josh asked, glancing toward Damon and the blood on the ground.

"Josh, please listen. It's important," she told him. "I will be in to talk to all of you together in just a few."

Josh slipped back inside, the door shutting gently behind him.

She had no idea what she was going to tell the kids, or how she was going to spin this, but she would have to keep

Andrew from getting in any further trouble. The stolen truck would be another issue, however.

They probably needed to call the detective and tell him everything that had transpired, but she was embarrassed by the thought. The last thing she wanted to do was talk about how and why she had found herself in the position she had with Damon and then the role she had played in allowing it to continue.

No matter what Sean tried to tell her about it not being her fault, and that Damon was simply a predator, she couldn't get past the fact that she had allowed him to bother her for so long. She wasn't a weak woman, but when it came to men like him, she wished she was stronger. The entire situation with him made her feel stupid.

Sean touched her arm. "Are you okay?"

She nodded, further upset by the fact that he could see her thoughts on her face so easily.

"If you want, the Springs has a car we can use until we can get your truck back." She motioned vaguely to where the van was parked behind the house. "It's not pretty, but it can get us around."

"Don't worry about the truck. I'll have Terrell start watching for it. The good news is that it was low on gas and my wallet is in my pocket. The kid will choke if he tries to gas up that beast."

She blushed.

Damon moved to get up.

"You just stay where you are." Sean pushed him back down to a seated position. "April, why don't you go inside and talk to the kids. I'll call Terrell and watch Damon until he stops bleeding."

She nodded, glad she wouldn't have to hear about her

failings as a counselor and a woman while he spoke to the detective and told him about what had happened and why. If she had stopped things earlier with Damon, and spoken to her supervisor at the house, maybe none of this would have even happened—hell, maybe she wouldn't have been on the mountain with Grace. Literally, everything bad that was happening was her fault.

"Good luck," she said, turning to go inside. "Please make sure to tell him that Andrew is a really good kid. This is not his normal behavior."

"Without a doubt."

She went inside and as the door closed behind her, she leaned against it and took a long breath. She needed to stop beating herself up for what was happening. Regardless of fault, there was nothing she could do to change the events that had transpired; all she could do was keep moving forward until she was through them.

There were the sounds of kids talking from inside the sunken living room down the hall. Josh was speaking, saying something about Damon, but she could only hear bits and pieces. Collecting herself, she moved slowly down the hall, not entirely comfortable with eavesdropping on the kids' conversation, but wanting to hear what was really happening in their world while it was completely unfiltered by their needs to perform for a counselor.

It was amazing how different they were when they thought someone wasn't listening.

"Damon has been hitting on her since she got here," one of the girls said, but she wasn't quite sure who was speaking.

"She liked it," Josh argued.

In that moment, she knew they had to be talking about her and Damon.

With that, she cleared her throat and made her presence known. She couldn't handle any more lashes from the whip of public opinion. "Hey, guys," she called a little louder than the situation required.

Several of the kids who had been standing hurried to chairs and sat down.

Josh was standing in front of the flat-screen television, and his hands dropped to his sides as she strode in. "What happened? Where's Andrew?" he asked, like he was the president of the Springs kids club.

"Andrew…" She paused, having no idea what she should say as heat rose into her cheeks. "He is fine, and hopefully he won't be in any trouble."

"So, he was the one who did that to Damon?"

"Yes. But violence is never the answer even when someone is verbally provoked." She was careful in how she spoke.

"Was this because of what he did to Grace?"

The warmth she had been feeling in her cheeks drained away as the blood started to seep out of her extremities and move straight to protect her core. "What?" she said, a chill moving over her skin. "What did he do to Grace?" she asked, each syllable punctuated by her instantaneous fear-induced anger.

Josh looked at a red-haired girl, Elyse, who had run with Grace before she'd disappeared. The girl wouldn't meet her gaze.

"Elyse, tell me. It's important." April moved gently toward the girl, trying to control her rage as she silently begged for her fears not to be realized. If Damon had laid a single finger on Grace…

"He didn't do nothing." The girl stared down at her pink toenails.

There were eight kids in the room. All of them were teenagers and had been through the ringer in their personal lives, but that didn't mean she could continue to question Elyse in the midst of them.

"Elyse," she asked, touching the girl gently on the shoulder in an attempt to get her to open up and feel comfortable with her. "Why don't we go talk somewhere away from everyone."

Elyse crossed her arms over her chest and flumped deeper in the couch cushion. "I'm not telling you anything."

April looked to Josh. "Would you please help me by taking everyone and escorting them to their rooms?"

Josh looked to Elyse, as if he was torn between wanting to protect her and at the same time knowing that he needed to listen to April.

"It's okay, Josh." She smiled as she gently squeezed Elyse's shoulder. "She is fine. We are all good. I just need to get a better understanding of what we are dealing with today."

It was one thing for Damon to have harassed her, but it was another thing entirely to potentially have taken advantage of children who had been entrusted to their care.

Hopefully she was just making more of this and the potential crimes he'd committed worse than what had actually taken place. Hopefully the kids just hated Damon. Hopefully...

So far, hope hadn't been working in her favor.

But maybe this time was different.

It took a couple of minutes, but the kids filtered out of the room. One of the other girls came over and touched

Elyse's other shoulder in what she could best assume was support.

There was something to be said for these kids. They had all been through hell and back, but when one of their own needed help, they were there. If for no other reason, she was glad to be a part of this world, a world where they could provide escape for the kids who had needed it the most.

Yet, if Damon had preyed on them, what good had they really been doing as a part of "the system"? What if by having these at-risk kids together in this home, they had created the perfect environment for a predator to easily find his prey?

Damon had to have just been bothering April. He couldn't have been targeting the girls here. He wasn't that bad, was he?

"Elyse." She said the girl's name like she was talking to a young child and not the surly teen who had every right to hate adults. "I need to know what you do about Damon and Grace."

Elyse turned her gaze toward the television even though it was just a black screen.

"Did Damon *touch* Grace? Ever?" The words curdled in her throat like soured milk. She hated that she had to ask such a question.

"What?" Elyse twitched. "No. No. Nothing like that," she replied, shaking her head vehemently.

Some of April's rage seeped from her. Maybe there was a ray of hope somewhere in this.

"Who were you talking about before I walked in? I think you said Damon had been hitting on *her* since she walked in. Did you mean Grace? Or did you mean *me*?" Again, the words stuck in her throat.

Elyse finally looked up at her, and she stared at her for

a long moment before she started to speak. "Come on. You know how it is here. We live by prison rules."

Maybe she had been naive, but she hadn't picked up on that dynamic with most of the kids—at least their full-timers. A few of the campers would come through jaded by life and hateful, but she'd treated them with love.

"What does that mean, Elyse?" she asked.

"It means that if we can work someone to get what we want when we want it, we are going to do it."

"What did you guys have to do to Damon to get what you wanted?" Her rage started to bubble up.

"Whatever it took. It wasn't his fault that we worked him. He was just an easy target." Elyse smiled, and the action was so unsettling that April was forced to look away.

She hated that these kids had to play games and manipulated people to get what they wanted. It wasn't their fault that they had learned to live this way, and she couldn't begrudge them for the role in having to play the game of survival, but she also didn't have to like it.

There were times when she had known the kids here had been testing her to see what they could get away with and how far they could take things. But she'd always been careful and considerate to set boundaries with their behaviors and their allowances. It came naturally to her, and it made her wonder what Damon was lacking in his life that they could have used for leverage to manipulate him.

"So, you guys were flirting with him?"

Elyse giggled, the sound so abstract set against the harsh reality of what was happening. "At first he would stop us, but when you guys broke up—"

"We were never really dating," she said, correcting the girl.

"That's not what he said."

"Hold up... He talked to you about *me*?" She really did hate this man. Didn't he know how inappropriate talking about his private life with teenage girls was?

"He wanted advice on how to get you in the sack. Well, not that he said that... He just wanted to know what kind of stuff you liked...you know?"

It disturbed her that he thought asking these girls was his best way to get information.

She didn't want to know what they told him. Everything about him made her disgusted. "So, you said *at first*, he would stop you from flirting. Does that mean that eventually he didn't? Was he flirting back with you guys?"

She shrugged. "I dunno."

"But he never touched you? Did he do anything else that you felt was inappropriate or out of line?" *Besides discussing our private life?*

She shook her head. "Not with me."

"But he did with Grace?"

"I don't know what they had going. It was weird, but I don't know if it was like dating or whatever." The girl shrugged. "When she talked about him, she said he was too old for her."

Now, Grace's actions during the rockslide and her hatred of her made more sense. Unbeknownst to April, they had been in some kind of cold war because of Damon. If Grace had just talked to her, she would have explained what an immoral piece of human garbage he was.

She had never believed in vigilante justice more than she did in this moment.

Whether or not he had physically harmed these girls, he'd wreaked havoc in their lives.

In allowing that, she and the system had failed.

"If you want to know who Grace really had a problem with," Elyse said. "Her foster parents."

April knew she was about to get a very necessary earful.

Chapter Seventeen

An hour later, Andrew still hadn't been found and they had been forced to call Terrell. Sean was standing with him outside, staring down the driveway in hopes the kid would return. Damon had gone back inside after Terrell had finished questioning him about the events earlier in the day. Of course, Damon denied knowing anything about Grace or why Andrew was upset, and he'd come out looking like a hapless victim.

The entire situation made Sean want to rage and fight, anything in his power to make things right. Yet, it kept feeling like they were coming up against roadblocks.

"I'm sorry," Detective Terrell said, leaning against the back of his black SUV. "From what you are telling me, Damon is a piece of work, and he shouldn't be working around kids, but he hasn't done anything I can arrest him for—April could hit him for harassment, but that would be about it." He dug the toe of his black boot into the gravel driveway. "Unfortunately, Andrew on the other hand... If either you or Damon wished to press charges..."

"Absolutely not," Sean said. He had a strong feeling, based on what he'd learned from April, that Damon wouldn't risk what the kids might reveal about him.

April came walking out of the front door of the house,

a red-haired girl by her side. She gave them a slight wave, as she made her way out to them. "This is Elyse, she's a really good friend of Grace's." She looked to the detective. "Elyse, do you wanna tell the detective what you told me about Grace's foster parents?"

Elyse looked over at April as if the last thing she wanted to do was talk to law enforcement. "I don't want things to get out of control. I mean, she didn't really even tell me much. Hell, I don't even know if what she told me was true. You know how Grace could be. For all I know she was just being dramatic."

Sean could understand all of the reasons the girl would want to minimize and downplay any information she had that pertained to the case. From what April had told him, the children who passed through the doors of this house were kids who typically had a great deal of experience with law enforcement and not always in the most positive ways.

This young lady probably had more insight into Grace's mindset than anyone else. Thankfully, though she appeared to be reticent, she seemed to be more helpful than Grace's other friends. Yet only time would tell.

"Elyse," Terrell said, "first of all just know that no matter what you say to me, neither you nor Grace will be in trouble. All we are concerned with is getting Grace back and making sure that she is safe and unharmed."

Elyse glanced over at April. "You guys think Grace was kidnapped or something?"

Terrell nodded. "Do you know of anyone else who would have wanted to take her, or harm her in any way?"

She shook her head. "The only people who Grace truly had a problem with were her foster parents." She paused. "She even told me that they had put a calendar up in their house marking down the days until they got the last check from the state for her care. They'd get really drunk sometimes, once even when I was there, and tell her all about how much they wanted her to just die."

Terrell frowned.

"Hold on a minute," Sean said. "If they were so wrapped up in getting money for taking care of her, then why would they want her to die?"

April made a slight choking sound, and he wanted to tell her it would be okay, but now wasn't the time or the place to indicate that they had anything more than a friendship type of relationship. The waters around them were murky enough without him allowing their own personal trauma to seep in.

Instead, he looked to April, and he gave her a slight nod, hoping she would see it as reassurance and could understand why he was holding back from further action.

"You know exactly why they treated her like they did," the girl said. "They're just like all the other foster parents out there. At least, all the foster parents I've ever come across. These people really don't care about us. All they care about is getting their monthly checks."

"Do you know when Grace's foster parents left the States?" Terrell asked.

The girl shrugged. "They were gone all the time. They left like two weeks before she went to camp, this round, but I honestly don't think they were around more than a week a month or so."

Terrell glanced over at him with a look of concern upon his face. He turned to April. "Did you know that these folks were not providing an adequate level of care?"

April shook her head. "I'm learning that I didn't know nearly as much as I thought I did."

Her statement made Sean's chest ache. "I think that's going around." He pursed his lips, as he hoped she would take some level of comfort in the fact that everyone was coming out of this situation humbled. The only hope that still resided was that Grace would make it through this situation alive.

If things continued the way they were, however, even that hope was minimal.

"Do you know where Andrew may have gone?" Terrell asked Elyse.

The question caught Sean off guard. He wasn't sure how Andrew's possible location was related to Grace's caregivers.

The girl wouldn't look at Terrell, but she shook her head. "I know he's upset with Grace. He thinks that she was egging Damon on with her flirtation, and he's not wrong. But I think he knows that Grace still loved him. She was just playing a dangerous game."

Terrell stuffed his thumbs in the edges of his vest near his armpits and sat quietly in thought for a moment. "Do you think Andrew still loves Grace?"

The girl pointed at the house, where Damon was sitting inside. "If he didn't, I don't think he would have done that to that guy's face. Andrew isn't one who is quick to get pissed off."

"Do you think that Andrew went to look for Grace?" Terrell asked directly.

"I'd put money on it." The girl glanced back at April. "Can I go back inside? I'm hungry."

April nodded. "Go for it."

"Elyse, I may need to ask you some more questions, please don't go too far," Terrell called after her.

She sent him a backward wave in acknowledgment.

The three adults watched as the kid retreated back into the house. Sean tried to tell himself that she was safe inside there, but his attempt to lie to himself was met with a mixture of feelings. Safety for any of these kids was tenuous at best… Hell, it was tenuous for everyone. Safety was never more than a hair's breadth away from becoming danger.

"What are we going to do?" April asked, crossing her arms over her chest. "We aren't any closer to finding Grace."

Terrell sighed. "No, but I've put out a MEPA, or a Missing and Endangered Person's Advisory, for her and I'll send one out for Andrew as well. You know, the kind of alert that you see on the television and social media sometimes."

"Don't those only last for twenty-four hours?" April asked.

"So, you do know a little bit about them?" Terrell asked.

"A little. We had a runaway a few years ago, but they ended up coming back after a day."

"Well, if Grace isn't found or doesn't come back, we can extend the advisory as long as we need. As you know, we use them in cases like this or where there have been parental custodial disputes that resulted in one parent absconding with a kid."

Though Sean had heard about custody battles, in his line of work, he wasn't privy to the ins and outs of the legal system.

Sean's phone rang. He pulled the device out of his pocket and stepped away from April and Terrell for a moment. Jim was calling. "Hello? What's up, man?"

On the other end, Jim cleared his throat. "How's it going? I hear you are light a truck."

Word traveled fast in a small town, a whole heck of a lot faster than he would have liked.

"Yeah, working on getting it back now." He tried to sound like he wasn't worried, but he was sure his friend had a pretty good idea of the emotional turmoil he was feeling without Sean having to tell him. "What's happening at the station? Everything good?" He glanced down at his watch. He wasn't supposed to be working until tomorrow at this time.

"Actually, I'm calling because I managed to pull a little bit more information from the fire scene. Do you have time to talk about it? It's nothing major, but I thought you'd like to know."

He looked over at Terrell, who was getting into his squad car and doing something on his computer. "Sure, what's up?"

"So, some of the lab work came back. I was right about it being diesel fuel. Which sent me down a rabbit hole today. So, I had them try to pull prints off the gas cap I showed you in the yard. I got a match."

"And?"

"This is where things get weird. The fingerprints came back as a match to your friend, April Twofeather. I think she may have started the fire."

Chapter Eighteen

April unlocked and opened the door to the Sulphur Springs' main office and slipped inside. The place was dark and though she had been granted access, it still felt as though she was somewhere she shouldn't have been. When she was working, she rarely had a need to come in here unless it was to talk with Brenda Dex, the director of the Springs.

She sat down at the desk that was pressed against the wall in the small office and picked up the phone to call Brenda, who was on vacation for a few days. Her phone went straight to voicemail. Carefully selecting her words, she let Brenda know about the situation with Andrew and what had happened with Damon—leaving out no details about his alleged flirting with campers and his using them to continue to harass her.

As she hung up, there was a chalkiness in her mouth. She wished she had the authority to fire Damon right now. He had no business continuing to be here and around the kids.

She was almost glad that Brenda hadn't picked up and she could just relay the details as they happened unencumbered by questions. She wasn't sure she was ready to talk about all the things Damon would have continued doing and the problems he would have created had things not been brought to a head.

Turning to go, she eyed the filing cabinet in a corner of the room. Inside was all the campers' and residents' personal information for the last few years. Opening the drawer, she pulled out the yellow file marked with Grace's name.

She scanned through the paperwork. From everything she had managed to pull up on Grace and her history, it appeared as though the girl had been in the system since she was put up for adoption when she was less than a year old. There wasn't an age that she was given up, or a date, but the documents noted that the parents were young and unable to provide care. Nothing more.

The words "young parents" jumped out at her as if in bold type. It was strange how a mind had a way of picking out the things that could hurt the most.

What if her daughter was out there somewhere fighting against the world like Grace was?

Her knees grew weak, and she was forced to sit down. Grace wasn't her daughter. Ann was. Ann had gone to a good home with a stable set of parents, probably in some tropical state where she was living her best life and growing up with stability, reliability and resources that, even now, April wasn't sure she could have provided.

These pervasive thoughts, the ones of guilt and the overwhelming sense of failure, had been a constant in her life, but she had been good at talking herself down from the ledge and keeping them at bay. Yet now, her normal composure and ability to compartmentalize were completely lost. Her emotions were out of control.

She needed to stay in check. If she didn't, she couldn't do her best for Grace. Every minute counted when it came to finding her. And, as they ticked by, feelings of desperation and failure were starting to seep in. Those cracks were just letting in every other feeling as well. She had to stay strong. She had to focus on the now and on doing everything in her power to get potentially helpful information.

Dipping her toes in the past wasn't helping.

She flipped to the next page in Grace's file. She'd been functioning at school, but according to her teachers was not performing to the best of her abilities. Which made sense, given that it appeared as though she was, for all intents and purposes, living on her own. Which meant the girl must have been working, but she didn't find any mention of Grace having a job or any form of steady income.

Perhaps that was why Grace hadn't tried to be emancipated from her current guardians. To do so, she would have to prove she had a good paying job and a stable place to live. Not to mention the fact that the girl likely didn't have the resources to seek legal counsel in helping her to remove herself from her situation.

If only Grace had spoken up and asked for help, April would have done everything in her power to extricate the girl from a bad situation.

She scanned through more of the background information the Springs had on Grace. Most of it was old medical records, nothing that seemed to have any bearing on her disappearance.

The next pages, however, were interesting. According to the paperwork the family had filed with the state, they had been fostering another girl as well—Summer Averian. The same Summer who she had last seen sitting out on the porch and refusing to answer their questions.

Why hadn't Summer told them that she was more than

just a friend of Grace's? More, that they had shared foster parents?

Summer had to have known that eventually the police looking into Grace's disappearance would find out and start to ask questions.

Then again, Summer had no reason to tell April and Sean the truth. They weren't the police, and they hadn't known what to ask. However, something about Summer not telling them the truth and speaking up when she had the chance felt strange. If nothing else, April would have to tell Terrell what she had found.

It was possible, and even probable, that he already knew. He had access to databases that had all of a person's information, including siblings, parents, known addresses and everything all the way down to every car they had ever owned.

Maybe she didn't need to tell him after all.

She closed the file, slipping it back into the cabinet. Stepping out of the office, she locked the door behind her.

The next shift of two counselors had shown up to take over for Damon, who'd been alone after the other counselor had called in sick. She could hear them talking in the kitchen when she walked by, but she didn't have any desire to take part in getting them up to speed. Regardless of how Damon wanted to spin this, the truth about him was going to come out—she'd make sure of it.

Hopefully Brenda would get the message before too long and Damon would never be allowed to set foot back on the grounds. Until then, she was going to steer clear of him—she didn't need him harassing her any more than he already had been since they'd met. He wasn't to be trusted.

The sun was bright as she walked outside, and it sat falsely against the darkness that was filling her soul. Sean was standing beside Terrell's vehicle, talking on his phone. He looked serious, and as he spoke she couldn't quite make out his words, but from the baritone of his voice she could tell he was angry.

She could only imagine what was happening now.

Sean looked up and he scowled as he looked at her. He quickly turned away.

Though she was sure it wasn't intended as a snub, his cold shoulder cut.

Terrell was in his car, typing on his computer.

She pulled out her phone, praying she would receive more information about Grace, but there were no new messages.

Walking over to Terrell, she gently tapped on his window to draw his attention. He looked away from his screen, closing it slightly, and he rolled his window down. "What's up?"

"I called the director and let her know what has happened." She paused. "I've been thinking—I want to file a report against Damon for harassment. Let's get the ball rolling for a restraining order. At the very least it will keep him away from here until Brenda can do a full internal investigation."

Terrell smiled. "You don't know how glad I am to hear you say that. Why don't you come on into the car, and I'll take your statement and write it up. From there, you'll need to talk to a Crime Victims Advocate who can help you get a temporary order of protection until you guys can get in front of a judge and make it more permanent, if necessary."

She nodded, but there was a sickening feeling in her stomach. She hadn't wanted to do this, but now it wasn't just her welfare at stake.

TWO HOURS LATER, after Terrell had dropped her off at the CVAs offices and she had filed her thirty-day temporary order of protection against Damon, she was relieved to finally be out in the fresh air again. It had been draining to go over everything that had happened between her and Damon, and then show proof of all the text messages and attempts he had made to contact her after she had written him off.

It wasn't going to be pretty when they went to court, but at least she had legal recourse if Damon attempted to contact her or try to get close to her. The only thing she feared now was the reality that often occurred when someone was slapped with a TOP—the violence and stalking behaviors escalated.

With any luck, Damon wouldn't go off the rails and he would see this as what it was—an attempt to make him realize his actions were out of line and that using children to get to her was absolutely despicable and couldn't continue.

As she walked outside, Terrell and Sean were sitting in Terrell's squad car, talking.

Sean had been *off* since everything had happened with Andrew, but they'd been so busy that they had barely had time to talk openly about what had gone on. Terrell gave her a tilt of the head and a smile, but Sean couldn't seem to meet her gaze.

"How'd it go?" Terrell asked, motioning her toward his window.

She lifted the copy of the papers the CVA had given her. "It's done. I have a hearing in thirty days. Until then he can't contact me or be within a thousand yards of me in any way." A sense of relief filled her, and a smile fluttered across her lips.

"That's great," Sean said, finally looking at her and smiling.

She hadn't realized how much she had needed his support. "Thank you, Sean. I'm glad you were here. I appreciate it."

He gave an acknowledging nod. "I'm glad you got it taken care of."

Yes, something with him was off. Everything he did and said just felt so *stilted*.

Was this because he had finally met Damon? He seemed in support of her taking the steps that she had to protect herself, but was he also judging her for allowing herself to get into such a predicament?

He didn't seem like the type to blame the victim, but maybe she was wrong in making that assumption.

Gah.

"Detective," she said to Terrell, "I know you're not a taxi, but I was hoping that maybe you could give us a ride back to my place. I'm *exhausted*."

Terrell sent a questioning glance to Sean that made her wonder what they had been talking about for the hour or so she had been inside the CVAs office.

"Sean?" he asked.

"Terrell and I were talking..." Sean started, but he seemed deeply uncomfortable as he shifted his weight and was entirely too preoccupied with a loose thread on the cuff of his shirt. "We both agree that it's probably not best if you go home. Damon is going to be served with the TOP sometime in the next day, and he may well come looking for you."

"I was thinking about that, too," she said, realizing that she hadn't really thought about Damon showing up at her door nearly as much as they had. "I guess I can get a hotel room."

Sean twitched and Terrell shook his head like they were having a completely wordless conversation. She hated feeling like she was being left out from whatever was happening, but at the same time maybe she was glad she didn't know what was going on. She already had enough to handle.

"How about you stay at my place?" Sean asked, but there was hesitancy.

"Sure." She tried not to notice it as all she really wanted was a safe place where she could get some rest. "But what about Grace?"

Terrell shook his head. "You guys don't need to worry about her tonight. I've got my people working around the clock, and we're going to look into a couple of leads we heard about today."

"What kind of leads?" she asked, a new sense of excitement filling her.

"Get in," Terrell said, clicking his computer shut and getting out of the car. He opened the back door for her. "I know it's not great to be seen riding around in the back of my car, but Sean's place isn't far. I'm sure no one will notice."

She was nearly certain someone would see, but she didn't care. Let the gossip mill run. It wasn't the first time she'd been the target of small-town chatter. As she got into the hard plastic, bucket-style seat, she clicked her seat belt into place. She tried not to think about all the people who had been cuffed, stuffed and escorted to jail in this seat.

The hard black seat bit into the back of her thighs as Terrell pulled out of the parking lot and onto the main road. The seat reminded her of sitting on a public bus, and it smelled about the same thanks to the scents of sweat, fear and bodies.

"So," she said, shifting her weight as she tried to get a better view of Sean and Terrell in the front seats through the hard Plexiglas window between them, "what new leads did you get?"

Terrell gave a quick glance back over his shoulder at her. "We've received two calls from our tip line. Like I said, I still need to follow up on them, but right now it sounds possible that Grace was spotted at a gas station in Bozeman."

"Who saw her?" she asked, wiggling with excitement.

"A gas attendant thinks he spotted her last night."

"Was she alone?" she pressed.

Terrell shrugged.

"What about the other call?" she asked.

It was quiet for a long moment, and the air conditioner fan and the road noise were the only sounds in the tight space.

"That one is a little more concerning. According to the caller, Grace was being trafficked to Chile to work as a housekeeper."

A housekeeper? She hoped that wasn't slang for something else, but the ache in her gut held her back from asking.

"Do you know who made the call?"

Terrell shook his head. "We didn't get a name, but we have the caller's phone information and last known location. I have a deputy out of Gallatin County working on that call as we speak." He pulled to a stop in front of Sean's house. "I'm going to run to Bozeman right now and link up with the other department. We'll go through their findings. If I get my hands on Grace or Andrew, I'll let you know. In the meantime…" He paused. "Please…stay safe."

Chapter Nineteen

Sean didn't want to leave April alone, but he also wasn't sure how he wanted to handle the situation with the gas cap. He hadn't told Terrell about the fire marshal's findings, and he wasn't entirely sure why. Perhaps it was the fact that he didn't want her to have played any kind of role in the fire.

No matter how many scenarios he went through in his mind, he couldn't make sense of how her fingerprints would have been on that cap. She had to have been the person who'd touched the plastic last, but there was no motivation for her to have torched Grace's foster parents' apartment. Well, except…maybe…if she had decided she hated Grace's foster parents for their having left her, but even that wasn't a good enough reason for her to burn down the one place Grace called home.

It just didn't make sense.

There had to be some reasonable explanation. She hadn't given him a reason not to trust her, in fact, quite the opposite.

The house was quiet when they walked in, and though he could understand why, he was a ball of nerves. It wasn't like they hadn't been alone before, and it wasn't like either of them were wishing to take things between them to another level.

"If you'd like, there's the guest bedroom. Or, you can have the couch," he said, motioning toward the place where he'd held her in his arms.

Things had gone haywire since he'd told her his truth, but he wished they could try again. She was everything he wanted in a life partner, but he couldn't help but wonder if they had gone through too much to come back from.

"What are we going to do without your truck?" she asked.

"I have an old Mustang in the garage. I haven't driven her in a month or so, but I know she has gas."

"She?"

He sent her a guilty grin. "She's fast, beautiful and a little temperamental."

"Should I be offended?" she teased with a gentle giggle.

"Not even a little, I was totally kidding. I really have no idea why I call it 'she.' It's just a habit I got from my dad."

Some of his nerves slipped away. She wasn't a criminal, and there was no way she could or would have done anything to hurt Grace.

Her smile faded, and he could tell she was thinking. After a moment, she turned to him. "Do you think we are going to get Grace back?"

"I want to think we will." He sighed, tired. "Do you want a drink or anything?"

"Sure," she said, but her smile didn't reappear. "Do you think the calls to the tip line were legitimate?"

He didn't want to tell her that she was probably right in being concerned on both fronts. She knew as well as he did that many of the calls that a tip line received were nothing more than prank calls, people with mental health issues or well-meaning folks who got it wrong.

He knew that in the case of Jim and his investigations, he often got dozens of calls and more often than not, they led to nothing. The only good news was that they only needed one real lead and they stood a chance.

"Terrell will get something from this. We just have to have faith in him." He grabbed two beers out of the fridge and smiled as he glanced over at the open bottle of wine from the other night.

It was strange how much things could change and evolve in just a matter of hours, and even minutes. Last week, he hadn't even considered having a woman in his life, and now he found himself silently begging that the red flags he saw in her were nothing more than decorations that might have matched his own.

He carried the beers out and handed one to her on the couch. She took a dainty sip and started to pick at the label. He felt the same need to keep his hands busy and as he sat down beside her he pulled at the silver corners of the label as well.

He glanced at her and caught her looking at him from under her eyelashes. Maybe history really did repeat itself.

He smiled at the thought.

"How's your arm feeling?" he asked.

She looked down at it like she had nearly forgotten about it. "It's a little achy, but fine. You know, I've never broken anything before."

His thoughts instantly shot back to the night Cameron had been killed. Sean had fared well, but he'd broken two ribs and sometimes when he worked out hard, they still ached. That had been the only time he'd broken bones, but he feared bringing it up. They had finally seemed to put the memory and pain of Cameron's loss behind them.

Then again, there was only sweeping it under the rug for moments, not forever.

"It wasn't your fault," she said, almost as though she could read his thoughts like they were headlines upon his face.

"Huh?" he asked, hoping he was wrong, and she was talking about something other than Cameron.

"His death." She sighed like she was resigned to the fact that they needed to talk about all the emotional pitfalls in the way of their being closer.

He grunted, noncommittal.

"If I've learned anything this week, it is that bad things happen to good people…especially to the kids and young people who have done nothing to deserve the hardships and losses they've been forced to endure."

"I deserve whatever happens to me. You can say it wasn't my fault, but—"

"You were a kid," she interrupted. "If your father hadn't shielded you, you would have been put through the wringer, too."

He looked at the silver label on the bottle. He still hadn't taken a drink. "Maybe you wouldn't have had to have gone through it alone if I had been made to pay for my role in his death."

"What role? You were just in the car. You were just a passenger. It was lucky he didn't kill you, too."

"That isn't entirely true. A deer jumped out. I yelled at Cameron to jerk the wheel. When he did, he was going too fast. We spun out and Cameron had overcorrected. It was my fault, April."

"You were doing what anyone would have done in that situation. Cameron was an inexperienced driver in the wrong place at the wrong time—and intoxicated. So were you."

She ran her hand over her hair, soothing herself. "There's no going back. There's no making different choices. I can't bring him back and neither can you."

He took a deep breath to control his guilt and pain. He had to be strong.

PISTON'S FOOTFALLS PADDED down the hall, breaking the silence as he thought about what April was saying. The cat rubbed against his legs, and he gave him a scratch before Piston did the same to April.

Piston purred as she touched him. He could understand the cat's reaction. Getting enough love, the cat disappeared behind the couch.

"So, I've been thinking…" she said, moving closer to Sean.

Her nearness made him inexplicably nervous. *What is she doing?*

She put her hand on his and looked up into his eyes. She was so incredibly beautiful. "You touched on it, but we can grow from these horrible things that have happened to us, together. We can find strength from one another on the days when we need it."

"We?" he asked, a smile trembling on his lips. He couldn't believe what he was hearing. She couldn't possibly be forgiving him—not after all the ways he had screwed up her life and caused her pain.

"Yes, we," she said, putting her hands on his face and looking him squarely in the eyes. "*We* can be together tonight. If you want?"

He took hold of her hands on his face and pulled one back, kissing her palm as he closed his eyes. There was nothing that felt quite like this, her skin on his. The scent of her hand, lavender soap with a faint hint of her perfume still on her wrist from this morning. He loved her smell. And he loved the way she made him feel.

"I want everything. I need *everything*," he whispered into the cup of her hand as he looked at her beautiful face. Her blond hair was caressing her cheek, and he took a strand of it between his fingers. It was nearly as soft as her skin. "Do you know how beautiful you are?"

She smiled. "I already said we could be together. You don't have to butter me up now."

He wanted to ask her what being together meant—she had first said for only tonight, but then just generally together. From the way she spoke about the future, it sounded as if she wanted a relationship. Maybe she was just as torn about them being together as he was. There were more reasons for them not to be an item than there were for them to try to make a relationship work, but at the core of his desire was his attraction for her.

He leaned in, moving his hands down her as he took her lips with his. Even her kiss was perfect. Her mouth yielded to his, but she was strong and passionate. Her tongue flicked against his, massaging him and teasing him.

His hand cupped her breast. Her bra was thin, and he could feel her nipple grow hard under his thumb. He wanted to take her nipple into his mouth and gently nibble as she moved to climax, but he wasn't about to rush the moment. Now, he wanted to make her moan his name— extra points if she breathed it into his mouth as his fingers explored the warmth between her thighs.

She reached down to pull her shirt over her head, but he stopped her with the touch of his hand. "I like to unwrap my own presents." He sent her a sultry smile. "Stand up."

She moved to her feet, but her movements were unsteady.

He took hold of the edge of her pants and pulled her closer to him so he could touch her soft belly with his lips. He loved her body. The way her curves pressed against the coarse fabric of her jeans. He pulled open the button of her pants, kissing the little red mark left behind by the confining button.

He took hold of her hips and pressed his face into her, kissing her hard as he took the zipper in his mouth and pulled it down. She giggled and it made him grin. He pulled her jeans down to her thighs. They held there, and he took his opportunity to sit back and stare at her white cotton panties.

"I should have changed," she said, pushing at her panties like she was embarrassed.

"I think they are perfect." He loved the feel of them on his mouth as he moved lower, pushing her jeans down and taking her into his mouth through her panties and sucking on the hard little spot he knew would drive her to ecstasy.

She threw her head back and grabbed his hair, pushing him harder against her. He hummed, tapping his tongue on her with his every break for breath. She tasted so good, like a mixture of pennies and sugar.

He pulled down her panties and licked her harder. Her legs started to shake as he pressed his mouth against her, using his chin to hit the other sensitive spots. He swirled his tongue, working figure eights of pleasure until her breaths quickened.

"I want to feel you inside me," she said, moaning.

"Am I doing something wrong?" he asked, pulling back from her.

"No." She shook her head. Her pupils were dilated and her eyes opened wide, and she pressed his head back down between her legs. "I…I'm close. If you keep going…"

Oh, hell yes…

He buried his face, letting her juices run down his chin as he moved with her body. He ran his fingers above her hard little spot, rubbing gently and flicking his tongue. She quaked, and he wrapped her in his arms as she released.

She called out, the sound echoing of the walls and settling deep in his heart. "Sean…"

Chapter Twenty

April woke up before him, and she rushed to the bathroom. Piston mewed lightly and, giving his head a good scratch. She cleaned herself up, then snuck back into Sean's bed, where they had finally come to rest after a night of love-making. He looked peaceful in his slumber, but she wasn't done. She would never get enough of him.

She slipped down under the sheets, taking him into her mouth.

"Mmm… Yes." He sucked in a long breath, gently waking as she moved up and down on him.

"April…" He said her name like it was a taffy, stretching and sweet on his tongue.

She moaned on him as she worked his hard, enormous length.

Everything about this man's body was perfect.

And don't get her started on all the things he could make her body do. He knew his way around a woman.

He lifted the sheets and smiled down on her, groggy. "Should I call you breakfast?"

She paused, taking him in her hand and stroking as she looked up at him. "What?"

"Well, you are going to be the first thing I eat this morning," he said, sending her a devilish grin.

She giggled, hard.

Taking it as a sweet weakness, he lifted her up to him and kissed her lips. "I hope you are ready for more," he said. "Get on your knees."

She followed his direction, her body ready for anything he wanted to do to her. He was a demigod in bed—complete with pecs that made her want to take a bite, and his abs were nearly washboard. Any more chiseled and she would have sworn he was made of stone and not right for a mere mortal like her.

He moved behind her and ran his fingers down her body, getting her used to his presence. Then she felt his tongue dip into her. She nearly lost control of her arms and she lowered her face onto the pillow, moaning as he kissed her gently on all the places he had played with last night.

His tongue flicked on her again, and as he played, she felt herself nearing closer and closer to the edge. When he ran his tongue over her and pressed it inside of her, the sensation was too much. She'd never experienced anything like it, and as he took hold of her hips and circled back to her mound with his tongue, she couldn't hold back.

He licked every drip from her as she quaked for him.

"That's my beautiful queen," he said, helping her move from her knees and laying her down. "Now, I'll make you your breakfast, my beautiful queen. You just stay here and rest. If things go our way, you are going to need your strength for more of this again tonight." He pushed her hair behind her ear and wrapped her in the sheet and light blanket. He started to get up, but turned back and gave her a playful smack to her butt, making her giggle.

"If you're lucky," she teased.

"I have a feeling that things are going to go my way."

He popped up from the bed like her body had been some kind of energy drink. She could hear him humming a song as he made his way down the hall and toward the kitchen.

He really was incredible.

She didn't know how she had gotten so lucky—not only had she found a man who was smart, kind, courageous and charming, but he was also her perfect match in bed. She'd heard about the unicorns out there who could make a woman howl and forget their names. Before last night, she wouldn't have believed it. Finishing had never come easily, until he had his way with her.

He had awakened parts of her that she thought were nothing more than urban myths.

She couldn't be more grateful, but hopefully she had pleased him in the same ways.

Her phone buzzed on the bedside table. *Ugh.*

It was fine. She could ignore it; it was still early.

It buzzed again, making her think about the Springs, Damon and Grace. There were too many things to worry about for her to bask in the glow of what she had just experienced and forget about the world— no matter how badly she wanted to.

It was an unknown number. Damon had been using unknown numbers, so she was fearful to answer, but if it was Grace then she would hate herself if she didn't pick up.

No matter what, Damon couldn't hurt her through a phone.

"Hello?" she asked, her voice rough.

"How could you?" Damon growled through the phone.

"Damon, I'm hanging up and I'm calling the police. You know you can't call me."

"Shut up. *You* know you don't feel like this. I know *he*

made you do this. You are mine. You've just been too... too *shy* to give yourself to me. And yet...you'll give yourself to him." He sounded hurt and furious.

She wouldn't have cared except for the fact that his knowing what had happened between her and Sean last night meant that he had been watching. The realization made goose bumps rise over her entire body.

"You...you have no right."

"You are the one who has no right. You are mine. You were mine before you were his, you are cheating—"

"I'm not cheating, Damon. I'm not yours. I've never been *yours*. I wouldn't be yours if you were the last man on earth. Why can't you understand?" Her words nearly choked her.

He laughed, the sound maniacal and high on the other end of the line. "That's fine... Just fine."

His laughter was terrifying.

"I'm going to hurt you, just as much as you've hurt me."

The line went dead.

She sat on the edge of the bed, staring at the phone in her hand. That couldn't have just happened, but it did. She should have known he'd break the order of protection and threaten her. Though she didn't want to, she would have to tell Sean and call the police and report what had just happened.

She had known that the threat of violence would escalate. Damon had never been well-adjusted, and her actions had definitely thrown him over the edge. She could only guess what he was going to do now. She wasn't safe anywhere she went.

If only she had trusted her gut when she'd first met this guy and not wanted to see the best in him. She felt so stupid and utterly terrified.

If she'd just kept him at arm's length, she wouldn't have had to file the restraining order or worry for her safety.

She captured a screen grab of the phone number and time of the call. It wasn't his number, or associated with his name, but her word would have to be enough. If something like this happened again, she would have to do things differently and record the call or something. She'd been in enough courtrooms to know that she'd need proof of his call and threat for the violation of the TOP to stand up in front of a judge. It would be her word against his in thirty days. He could easily deny that he'd called and threatened her.

She looked at the window. What if he was just outside and waiting for her to stand up so he could shoot her through the glass? At least there wasn't a car parked outside for him to booby trap. That was one less worry.

There were the sounds of Sean cooking coming from down the hall. He was still humming. Just like that, she was going to ruin his day and crush his feeling that things were going to go his way. By now, they should have both known better than to call up the fates by speaking hopes aloud.

She quickly got dressed and slipped to the window, staying behind cover as she carefully looked outside. From where she stood, she didn't see Damon or his car, but it didn't bring her much comfort. He wouldn't have been so stupid to be out in the open if he was going to try to kill her.

Then again, he wasn't smart enough to take a hint or follow police orders.

She pushed the curtains closed, careful to avoid putting her arm out in the open.

It struck her that this was how things were going to

be. She would always be afraid and waiting for the bullet to strike.

What kind of life would this be if she was living in constant fear?

She checked herself. For now, it was *her* life. She was going to have to fight to keep it.

Sean smiled widely at her as she made her way out into the kitchen. "Hey, babe," he said, leaning over to her and giving her a kiss on the cheek. "Breakfast is about ready." He motioned toward the scrambled eggs with the spatula in his hand.

"Did you just hear me in there?" she asked, motioning toward the bedroom.

His smile grew impossibly wider. "Oh, I heard you all right." He laughed, but as he looked at her face he abruptly stopped.

"No." She shook her head and lifted her phone slightly so he could see what she meant. "Damon just called."

He stopped moving. After a long moment of silence, he turned away from her and carefully put the spatula down and turned off the stove. "Let's go."

She wasn't quite sure what he meant. "Where?"

"Let's run to the police station. We will file a report and have his ass brought in for violating his TOP."

He hadn't even asked what Damon had said; it was like he already knew. She appreciated not having to explain it to him. He probably knew that whatever Damon had said wasn't something he wanted to hear or give attention to.

Grabbing the keys that were hanging on the wall by the door leading to his garage, he motioned for her to follow him. She wasn't sure what she feared more, Damon or Sean's eerie silence.

The mustang was a pearly opalescent white and it sparkled in the sun as he opened the garage door. He moved to the passenger side and opened her door. She climbed in, almost afraid to speak.

It wasn't until they were approaching the police department that Sean finally made a sound. "I've been meaning to ask... Jim brought something up to me..."

"The fire marshal?" she asked.

He gave a stiff nod. "He located fingerprints on the gas cap we found at Grace's apartment." He slowed to a stop at the light. No other cars were around, and he turned to face her. His eyes searched her face in a way that made her deeply uncomfortable. "Was there anything about the fire at Grace's that you haven't told me?"

"No." Her stomach ached. "Why?"

"It was *your* fingerprints."

She stared at him, trying to make sense of what he was saying to her and all that it implied. "You don't think I *actually* had anything to do with the fire at Grace's, do you?"

He ran his hand over his face like he was trying to wipe away wayward thoughts. "No. I have been going over it and over it since he brought it to my attention. I just want to make sure that I'm right."

"The last thing I want to do is cause Grace more heartache," she choked out. "Hell, all I've wanted to do is help her—since the moment she and I met." Her anger roiled within her, making heat rise up from her core. The mere thought that someone could think she'd intentionally hurt a kid made her want to scream.

"If I thought you had anything to do with the fire, or if you were the kind of person I had to worry about, last night wouldn't have happened. I'd like to think I have a pretty good idea of the incredible woman you are, but I had to tell you about the fingerprints." He extended his hand, and she slowly put hers in his.

She wasn't sure how she felt; there were so many things going through her mind right now...but at the center of it all, she held no doubts that Sean was there for her. He was the one person in her life who was safe.

"Do you have any clue how your fingerprints would have been there? Did you fill a gas can anytime recently?" He squeezed her hand as though he was trying to reassure her.

She thought back to the last time she'd even held a gas can. "I bought some diesel for the camp's lawn tractor a week ago. I normally don't mow, but they gave me a bonus if I did it, so..."

"There we go. Grace probably stole the can from the group home," he said. He pulled to the right, instead of continuing to go toward the station. "Let's swing by your apartment." He motioned to her phone. "Why don't you go ahead and text Terrell and let him know about the thing with Damon and that we will be dropping by to file a report."

She sent a text off to the detective, careful to include the picture she'd taken of the phone number and carefully quoting what Damon had said. As she typed, bile rose in her throat.

What if Damon was following them? He had made it clear he'd been watching her. She glanced up from her phone, but she didn't see anyone but a lady out watering her flowers.

"Sean," she said, trying to quell the fear she was feeling and not let it leak into her voice, "Damon said he was going to hurt me. If he's following us..." She motioned her chin in the direction of her apartment, just minutes away.

"If he's there, then he will have to deal with me."

She wanted to point out that Sean didn't have a gun. What was he going to do if Damon came at them with a weapon? She wanted to feel completely protected with Sean by her side, but her anxiety was weighing on her. There were too many variables—and the one common denominator was unpredictability.

Chapter Twenty-One

As he turned the corner and April's apartment building came into view, the first thing he spotted was his pickup truck.

"What in the hell?" he said, pointing toward his truck.

She looked up from her phone. "Oh…"

He pulled to a stop beside it, hoping that Andrew would be inside. He was nowhere to be seen outside the building.

"Why do you think he came here?"

Sean shrugged. "I'm hoping that he knew we'd find the truck if he dumped it here."

April nodded. "I told you. Andrew is a good kid. He just needed a way to escape."

It would have been nicer if the kid had dropped it off at his place, but he doubted that Andrew would have known how to find him, or his address. Which made him think. "How did he know where you lived?"

April shrugged. "I have no idea."

He knew she thought of Andrew as a good kid, but the teenager had kicked the living snot out of Damon. Which meant he was capable of violence.

"Let's go inside and check on things," he said, turning off the car and getting out.

She motioned to her apartment door, which was slightly ajar. "I know I locked it when I left the other day."

They walked toward it, but before he had even gotten close, he could see that dead bolt had been broken and the inside of the door frame was dangling loosely just inside the door, which was keeping it from closing.

He didn't dare to touch it. "I think we need to get Terrell over here."

She was already tapping away on her phone. In a few moments, she said, "He'll be here in ten." She snapped a picture of the lock and the door and sent it off to the detective. "There."

"Let's take a look inside your apartment and see if Andrew's behind this." *Or if Damon or someone else had broken in.*

Her face blanched slightly. "Don't you think we should wait for Terrell or a deputy? Damon…"

"Probably didn't do this," he said, motioning toward his deserted truck. He touched her arm. "You're fine. Everything's fine." Even as he spoke, he wasn't quite sure that he believed himself. "Let's just go take a quick look."

He pushed open her door. There, stuck inside the wall by the light switch, was a note. It simply read: "I'm sorry. I have to find Grace. —A"

The poor kid. He felt for Andrew, he really did. If he had a chance, he would have assured him that he and April would stand by him if he was worried about getting in trouble for fighting and running away, and that they *all* wanted to find Grace, in every sense of the word. Everything Andrew had done was understandable, especially given his age.

"Well, I think he's proven that he's not the kind of kid without a conscience," he said, pulling the note off the door and handing it to April.

"I tried to tell you that before."

They went inside. Even though the door had been slightly ajar, the place held the stale smelling air that came with enclosed spaces and summer heat. Masking it, though, was the sweet scent of her perfume.

Her apartment was clean and meticulously organized, even the mail on the counter was sorted by size, largest to smallest. "I'm guessing everything is undisturbed?" he asked.

She walked over to the kitchen island where the pile of mail sat waiting for her. She picked up the envelope on top and flipped it over, reading the back. "So far, except the door, we are good."

They walked back toward her bedroom. As he followed her there was the sound of breaking glass behind them in the living room, and then a distinctive *whoomph.*

He instantly knew that noise.

Fire.

His realization was met with the faint aroma of gas.

There was an explosion, and as he turned, the heat of the gas-fueled flames blasted against his face. His eyelashes curled from the heat. As if time had slowed, he turned back to April and threw himself on top of her as the fire rushed overhead at them. It was only a millisecond, but it could have been a minute as he watched her fall to the floor under his body. He pressed her down as the fireball ballooned over them.

"Are you okay?" he called to her.

She nodded, but her eyes were wide with terror.

"Stay low," he ordered. "Move toward your room as fast as you can. I'm right behind you."

She nodded, army-crawling the distance to her room,

using her pink cast as well as she could. The air was thick with smoke, and he could detect the faint smell of burned hair…likely his own.

They didn't have long before the smoke would overtake them. It was a matter of minutes. In events like these, time worked in mysterious ways. There were instances when he'd been donned up, masked and working that it had felt like he'd been in a building just a matter of seconds when in fact he'd nearly run out of air in his tank. And then, there were times like these when seconds felt like forever.

Though he knew she was moving as fast as she could, he needed her to go faster. As he moved to speak, there was a strangled cry from her second bedroom.

"April?"

She looked back at him.

"Was that you?"

She shook her head.

There was someone else in this apartment.

"Call out if you need help!" he yelled.

The fire roared around them, but he heard a man's voice. He was calling for help, but his words were muffled by the closed door and the sounds of the fire.

"Is there a window in your back bedroom?" he asked April, motioning toward the room.

She shook her head and stopped moving to talk to him.

"No! Keep moving. Don't stop. I want you to get to your bedroom and get out that window as fast as you can."

She wanted to say something, to argue, but he shut her down. "Move. Now. Go!"

She hustled forward turning the corner into her bedroom. He moved behind her, closing the door to her room in an attempt to stop the smoke from getting any heavier in there, but in doing so it immediately made the smoke downdraft toward him, filling his lungs.

He coughed, fighting the terror that rippled through him. That had been a mistake, but he didn't care as long as she got out. She came first. Not him. He'd promised to protect and keep her safe. He was going to stand by his word, no matter the cost.

The smoke thickened around him, and he tried not to breathe, but his coughing fit had cost him, and he could feel the smoke burn at the insides of his lungs.

He forced himself to get lower, his face almost on the carpet as he moved toward the second bedroom. The door was closed, and he reached up, grasping blindly until he found the handle. Twisting it, he pushed it open. The smoke from the hall cascaded like billowing water into the room.

There was another *whoomph* sound as the oxygen from the room met the flames, feeding them. He rushed into it the bedroom, closing the door behind himself hoping that it would stop the fire and smoke from its rapid advance.

"Hello?" he called, using his sacred breath to help this unknown man.

"Help!"

He followed the man's call and found him huddled in the corner of the room, against the back wall and across from the bed. As he drew close, he recognized Andrew's face immediately.

What was he doing in here? Why was he hiding? His note said he was out looking for Grace, but he must have surprised him when he'd been leaving the note. Maybe the kid had been trying to hide.

Sean was mixed with a sense of relief and terror for the boy who sounded all too much like a full-grown man.

Andrew was breathing hard, pulling way too much smoke into his lungs. A tear was running down his cheek.

"Are you okay?" Sean asked.

The kid nodded, but he could tell something was wrong. As he opened his mouth to speak, Andrew started coughing.

Sean glanced around the smoke-filled room. Through the haze, he spotted a bottle of water on the table near the bed. He rushed to grab it. He pulled his shirt over his head and doused it with the water. He threw the empty bottle on the floor.

"Andrew, take this shirt and loosely put it over your head and around your mouth and nose." He handed the kid his shirt.

He wrapped it around his head as Sean had instructed. "Okay, we are going to move to the other bedroom. There's a window there, we can crawl out. Okay?"

Andrew nodded.

"I want you to stay close to the floor, as close as you can get while moving as fast as you can. Okay?"

Andrew nodded again.

"All right, kiddo, let's go." He moved toward the door. The smoke in the room was stinging his hurting lungs, and he tried to control his breathing.

He would be okay. They'd all make it out of this fire alive.

This was his job.

He kept checking over his shoulder to make sure that Andrew was following him through the smoke. There was a cord on the floor, and he yanked at it, pulling it from the wall. The small lamp it was attached to crashed to the ground. He took hold of the lamp and handed the end of the cord to Andrew.

"Out there," he said, motioning toward the hall, "it's going to be impossible to see. You need to keep hold of this. I'll lead us out. Got it?"

Andrew nodded as he looped the cord around his wrist.

Everything is going to be okay, he told himself. As he did, he was reminded of his telling April that exact same thing not all that long ago. Even then, he hadn't been sure everything would be okay, and he was even less sure now, but he had to calm himself.

He had enough experience. He'd been through hundreds of fires and training environments. None were exactly like this, but they were close. He just needed to keep his emotions in check and allow his muscle memory and training to take over.

Tapping the door handle to make sure it wasn't too hot, he then turned the knob. His body was instantly flooded with heat and the stinking, acrid smoke of the house fire. In the few moments he'd been in this room with Andrew, the fire had taken over. Though he couldn't see the flames because of the black, tarry smoke, he could feel the heat of the active flames overhead.

Though he knew April's bedroom door was close, his heart thundered in his chest as he blindly swept his hands on the floor, trying to find where it met the carpet. He edged forward, finding the wall and moving down it. The wall was warm and gritty from smoke and ash.

He tried to keep his breathing as slow and metered as he could, but his heart was racing, and he found himself struggling to win the battle against nature.

He reached up and tapped the doorknob. It was hot and stinging, but he didn't have a choice. He moved fast, twisting the knob as it burned his fingers, and he forced the door open and tugged on the cord. Andrew moved closer, and he brushed against his foot as he rushed into the room.

Glancing around the room, he was semiblinded by the smoke, but he didn't see April. Her bed sat at the far side of the room and her closet was open. Everything seemed in place. He looked up and watched the smoke pour out of the bedroom window. Helping Andrew over the edge, he lifted him outside and into the fresh air. He followed, slipping over the windowsill, and scraping down the siding of the building until he hit the sidewalk.

Getting his feet on solid ground outside of a fire had never felt better. He took a deep gulp of air and tried to blink away the stinging in his eyes. His lungs felt like he'd smoked three packs of his grandmother's cigarettes. He hacked, trying to take a breath that didn't ache.

Andrew walked into the parking lot, pulling the shirt from his face. The areas of his head that hadn't been covered by the wet cloth were covered with dark soot, and his eyelashes were caked with ash.

Sean could guess how he looked after crawling all over the floor. His chest was sweaty, and he touched his skin. It felt gritty with dirt and ash. His fingers ached with burns, but all in all he was going to be okay.

"April?" he called, looking around the parking lot.

There was no answer.

She had to be outside. She had to have gotten out. The window was open. There was no one else in the bedroom.

He panicked.

Was she still in there? Had she gone back in?

"April!" he yelled, hoping she simply hadn't heard him.

He started back toward the window. On the siding near

the bottom of the window was a small, bloody handprint.
One too small to be a man's. It had to have been April's.

He called her name again; he sounded frantic.

There was still no answer.

April was gone.

Chapter Twenty-Two

What in the hell?

April had no idea where she was or what had happened. She remembered she had been coming out of her bedroom through the window. Something hit her. It hit her hard in the head. There was pain. So much pain. And blood. She remembered the blood.

A blindfold covered her eyes, but she guessed she was in the trunk of a car as she heard the muffled sounds of a radio and road noise beneath her. They hit a bump, and it threw her up in the air a couple of inches before she came down hard on what must have been the scratchy industrial carpet lining the area.

Her hands were tied together in front of her. Reaching up, she touched the tender spot on the back of her head where there was an open cut.

There was a pounding in her head.

Using her bound hands, she rubbed at the blindfold on her eyes, slipping it up on her forehead. It was pitch-black around her, but she was less afraid than she had been when she'd been blindfolded.

She listened hard to try to make out the sounds of anyone talking, hoping to identify who had taken her. Instead, the stifling hot air of the trunk seemed to grow impossibly hotter, and it amplified the sickening scent of smoke that had been on her skin.

It had to have been Damon who had taken her. There was no question in her mind, even though she hadn't heard anything to confirm. He drove a late-model Toyota Corolla. It had a small trunk, and as she stuck out her legs, they jammed into the sidewall of the trunk before she could even extend them.

Yes, it had to be Damon's car.

The police must be looking for him. They had to know he started the fire. At least, as long as Sean had gotten out of the apartment. He had been right behind her.

Did he know she was gone?

That she had been kidnapped?

If he did notice, how long had it taken before he'd realized?

She was flooded with questions as she tried to make sense of the situation in which she found herself.

Yet, she couldn't worry about that. She needed to come up with a plan to get out of this trunk. Or, what to do when Damon would finally stop to let her out.

He had to be taking her somewhere to kill her.

The only luck she'd had in this was the fact that he hadn't pulled the trigger when she was coming out the window. If he'd wanted to, that would have been the perfect opportunity. She'd had her back turned. She was focused on just getting out of the fire alive.

He had set the whole damn thing up.

The worst part was that she had known he had been gunning for her, and yet he had still gotten the drop on her.

She'd never thought he would actually do something like this. He hadn't been homicidal. Pathetic, yes. Needy, yes.

Manipulative, yes. But why, if he professed to love her so much, would he have wanted her dead?

Maybe he didn't intend on killing her. Maybe he just wanted to kidnap her for his own use.

She wasn't sure which would be worse.

No matter what his plans were, she was going to fight like hell.

EVERY FEAR HE'D ever held was being realized in a single second.

Sean sat on the edge of the sidewalk watching his team as they battled the blaze at April's apartment complex.

The black smoke curled up into the sky, filling what would have been a beautiful blue-sky day with dark clouds.

He sniffed at the air but couldn't smell anything but the smoke that had penetrated his lungs. The EMS worker was standing over him, making sure he kept on his oxygen mask as he tried to control his emotions. The woman looked down. "How are you feeling?"

He couldn't tell her that he was scared out of his mind. That he felt like a failure. That he'd never forgive himself if April had somehow gone back into the building and he'd missed it.

"I'm going to be fine." He motioned to the kid who was lying on the gurney inside the ambulance with his eyes closed. He looked almost asleep. "How's Andrew doing? Did everyone make it out okay?"

"Everyone made it out and is going to be fine. We are going to run Andrew to Bozeman to receive care." She reached into her pocket. "He asked me to give you these." She handed him his truck keys. "And to tell you he was sorry." She made her statement sound like a question, but he didn't want to go into the details with her as he took the keys.

"Was anyone else outside when my crew got here, do you know?" he asked, his voice was raspy, and he had to suppress a cough.

She shook her head. "I have no idea. Why?"

Someone had tried to kill them *that* was why. "Did anyone see a vehicle leaving the scene around the time the fire started?"

The EMS worker shrugged. "You'd have to ask the police officers." She motioned down the road.

In the distance, he spotted Detective Terrell. The guy looked deadly calm, which only meant one thing in their first-responder world—it was go time. Things were getting real. Now, he was truly terrified.

"If I promise to keep on my mask, can I walk over there?" he asked, motioning toward Terrell.

She nodded and handed him the green oxygen tank.

He walked over to Terrell and the detective gave him a deep tip of the chin in acknowledgment. He put his fingers up, motioning for the officer he was talking with to be quiet.

"Did anyone see anything suspicious at the scene?"

Terrell turned toward him. "We have a car matching the description of Damon's leaving the area. They couldn't see who was driving, but I think it's safe to say it was likely Damon. I've put out a BOLO for him. Highway patrol will be on the lookout for him if he tries to leave the area, but he may have gotten past them already."

He nodded. As much as he wanted to tell them to shoot to kill if they saw the bastard, he stayed quiet. "Besides, Damon had April. They'd all have to be careful."

"Andrew looks a little worse for the wear." Terrell motioned toward the ambulance. "I'm going to try to talk to him as soon as Brenda gets here from the airport—she came home early from vacation when she heard what happened. She said she'd meet us at the hospital. Did Andrew say anything to you?"

Sean shook his head. "Just that he was sorry."

Terrell's features darkened. "I'm sure he is. Anything else? Anything as to why he was in the apartment at the time the fire started?"

He hadn't realized until right now that from the detective's perspective, it made sense to think that Andrew was likely the one who had set the place ablaze. Sean clearly hadn't explained the situation well enough. "He was hiding in the back bedroom when I was trying to get April out."

"And she came out of the window before either of you?" he asked, even though he'd already given the guy a brief about what had happened when the EMS workers had started treating him.

"I thought she did, yes."

"So, you know for a fact that she didn't go back into the apartment?"

He popped his neck, purely out of stress. "I don't think she went back inside. I think Damon took her. He threw the bomb into the house. Hell, he probably started the fire at Grace's, too. He seems to have a thing for fire."

Terrell's features went impossibly darker. "I hear what you are saying, Sean. The thing is, Damon had an alibi for the time that the fire was started at Grace's apartment— he was working at the Springs. The kids reported seeing him. He couldn't have been the one to set it."

"Okay..." He felt the wind leave his sails. "That doesn't

mean he didn't have something to do with these fires…
and April's going missing."

Terrell nodded, but the action was placating. "Jim told
me that the prints he found at Grace's fire came back as
April's."

"Yes, she had filled up a gas can the week before. She
had mowed the lawn at the group home."

"I got the video records for the gas station nearest the
Springs, and I did manage to find her filling it up as she
said."

"I'm not surprised," Sean said. "She has no reason not
to tell you the truth."

"Yes and no, Sean." Terrell shifted his weight like he
was about to throw a bomb. "According to some of the
folks where she worked, she and Grace did not get along.
They had a very antagonistic relationship."

"I would venture to guess that most of the kids didn't
get along with authority figures there. Did you talk to Andrew? Andrew loves April, and he knows just as much as
I do that she wouldn't have done anything to hurt anyone
in her care."

"Did she tell you that Grace is her biological daughter?"

What in the actual hell?

"No. Grace isn't her daughter. There's no way."

Terrell arched his brow. "I spoke to Damon after you
left the house last night. He was the one who told me. He
had the adoption paperwork from both sides on his phone.
He made it sound like April knew all about Grace. Are you
saying she didn't tell you or you think she didn't know?"

"I swear, I don't think April knows." How did *Damon*
know?

"Really?" Terrell looked surprised. "You think she

wouldn't have had access to the same files as Damon? That she wouldn't have put it together?"

"How did Damon get the files?"

Terrell shrugged. "He didn't say, but the paperwork was notarized."

He thought about the strange situation between her and Damon. Was this what he was holding over her head and why she hadn't wanted to move against him and get the TOP until he'd forced the issue? Was it possible that she was afraid that Damon would tell Grace that she was her birth mother or vice versa?

If Grace had known the truth, perhaps that was part of the reason she had disappeared. But that didn't help Sean make sense of the strange, garbled phone call they had gotten from Grace.

"Did you actually look into Damon's documents? Wouldn't that be something you would have access to through your database, NCIC?"

"Adoption records?" Terrell shook his head. "Absolutely not. Those are sealed by the courts in most cases."

Then how did Damon get his hands on them? "Can you get the documents?"

Terrell sighed. "Maybe, but in this case, I think we need to focus on finding Grace and April."

"Are you going to arrest April?" he asked.

He wasn't sure if working with Terrell would be in his best interest if the man was going to arrest her for a role he knew with almost complete certainty she didn't have in the fire. However, Sean had questions and there was a tiny bit of doubt within him because he didn't know what was going on with April. What she knew or didn't know. Yet, even at the thought of the possibility that April had started the fire at Grace's, he found that he was shaking his head. There could be some kind of motive there, but this was a case of Damon trying to clear his name and create a shadow of doubt to avoid trouble.

Terrell was watching him. "I just need to talk to her and see what she has to say about her fingerprints being at the scene of the arson. I also need to see if she had any desire to harm Grace."

He opened his mouth to argue that April had been in the hospital when Grace had initially gone missing. There was no way she could have kidnapped the girl.

"Before you say a word, think about it…" Terrell put up his hand. "We all know not to go up on that mountain in those kinds of conditions. I'm not saying April set up the slide, but she was an avid hiker—I'm sure you can see why I'm concerned. And while she may not have kidnapped Grace initially, I believe she may have known Grace had returned to her apartment—there, the girl was a captive target."

"April was with me the whole time."

"When I questioned Damon yesterday, he told me you'd say that. He also said she wasn't above getting someone to do her dirty work."

"Damon is the one who you should be digging into, not April. She has an alibi. April wouldn't hurt anyone."

"Just like you wouldn't?" Terrell countered.

His sharp words stabbed deep. "What do you mean?"

"Damon told me about you and your role in your high school friend's death."

"I didn't kill him. I didn't hurt him. I was just in the car."

"That's not what Damon said."

"That case was closed. I was cleared."

Terrell nodded, but he studied him. "And your father

was who he was—you and I both know your dad pulled strings. I know how these things work. Your father didn't want you to ruin your life. One kid was dead, another one was looking at a possible court battle. He did what he needed to do."

"Screw you, Terrell," he said through gritted teeth. "You know I was just a kid in the wrong place at the wrong time. My father was a good man. Don't discredit his memory or me based on some stalking jerk's word. Damon's the one who you need to dig into—not some stupid conspiracy theory he tried to get you hooked up on. You know how these games are played…he's a con man."

Chapter Twenty-Three

April waited until the car came to a stop and the engine turned off. From the earlier sounds of the tires and the number of ruts, they had to have been somewhere on a gravel road. Her heartbeat was thrashing in her ears, muffling the car door as it slammed shut. The car bounced and a second door slammed shut.

There were two. Two people who wanted her dead.

They were going to kill her.

They were going to get rid of her body deep in the woods where only the bears and vultures would find her.

Her emotions welled in her throat, and she tried to swallow them back. She was going to have to fight. She pulled at the paracord that was tied tight around her wrists with her teeth, frantically trying to get free. All her pulling did was yank the cord tighter and make her hands tingle from a lack of blood flow.

She twisted her hands, trying to loosen them. But her captors had tied the knot through the thumbhole in her cast. As she pulled, the hard cast rubbed her skin raw.

Thankfully her feet hadn't been tied. She could kick.

Or, what if she played dead?

What if they opened up the trunk and had a gun in their hands? One pull of the trigger and she'd be gone.

There was the jingle of keys and footsteps approaching the trunk. A key slid in the lock and ground as the teeth clicked into place. The trunk popped open. The slit of light blinded her and burned her eyes, and she was forced to close them for a moment.

Silhouetted by the sun was a dark shadow of a person. From the round shape of the body, it was a woman. A thin breeze kicked up, filling the stagnant air of the trunk with fresh air. As the wind blew, the woman's green hair lifted and shone in the light, giving her a strange swamp-colored aura.

Grace.

The fight left her body. What was Grace doing here?

"What... Grace? Why?" she stammered.

The girl grabbed her ankles and swiveled her legs out of the trunk. "Just be quiet."

There was another set of footfalls as someone walked around from the driver's side.

"Stand up," Grace ordered.

April wiggled forward, struggling to sit up with her legs arched over the metal edge of the trunk. Grace grabbed her arms and pulled her up, her thighs scraping on the plastic weather stripping and scratchy industrial carpet. Grace's fingers dug into her flesh as she tried to right herself and find her balance.

Damon stepped around the back of the car. "How was your ride?"

She couldn't stand looking at Damon's weasel face, with his long, crooked nose and beady little dark eyes. She hated him with every cell in her body.

"Grace? What are you doing with him?" Her words came out as whispers. She couldn't believe it.

Didn't Grace know what kind of man she had found herself with?

She glanced down at her bound hands.

Grace had to have known. She was complicit. She had kidnapped her. *They* were going to kill her.

"Why?" April asked, trying to sound stronger and more dangerous than she felt. "What do you want from me?"

Damon smiled, and tendrils of saliva stuck to his bottom lip from his canine teeth, reminding her of the predator he was. "I want everything from you. Do you know how much you've hurt me? What you've done? You've ruined my life."

She looked to Grace, who was looking adoringly at her mentor.

"I...I'm sorry, Damon," April said, playing along in an attempt to mollify the crazed man. "I didn't mean to hurt you. You were just...*scaring* me." She tried to look coquettish and supplicating.

His spine softened and he licked the saliva from his lip. "I didn't mean to scare you. All I ever wanted was for you to know how much I cared about you. How much *I love you*."

Her thoughts instantly moved to Sean. He was the man she wanted to love her. He had to be searching for her. She silently called to him, hoping he would feel her soul reaching out.

She glanced around, trying to figure out where in the world they had taken her.

"Do you love me, too?" Damon pressed. He reached forward and took her hand, lifting her bound fingers.

She nodded, afraid that if she tried to speak those words aloud to him that she'd retch.

"I knew that Sean had made you act the way you did."

He picked at the rope on her wrists. "If I untie you, will you behave?"

She nodded, clamping her lips shut.

Hate filled her, taking the place of the fear she had been harboring. This man was nothing to fear. He was no longer human; he was nothing more than the embodiment of all the judgments, opinions, dismissals, pettiness, overt hatred and lies everyone in her life had ever placed upon her. He was just something she had to conquer. She would.

He took a knife out of his front pocket and gingerly placed the tip under the rope and started to saw next to the knot. The knife was dull, and it struck her how ill-prepared the man was if he was going to hurt her.

It made her wonder if he'd not planned her kidnapping or if it had been more of a desperate act by a desperate man.

Or, maybe, Grace had been the brains behind this.

She looked over at the girl. There was something familiar in her eyes—if she had to guess what it was, it was resolve. This girl was determined to do something, but she wasn't quite sure what. All April could hope was that it wasn't to murder her. Because she wasn't already dead, she had to guess the odds were in her favor.

As he cut her loose, the rope fell from her wrists. She turned slightly and there, lodged in the corner of the dark trunk, was her phone. It must have fallen from her pocket when they'd put her in the trunk. She looked away as quickly as she could so as not to draw their attention to the device.

"I have to use the restroom," she said, saying the first thing that she could think of in order to get a moment alone.

"She's fine," Grace argued.

Finally, the girl had found her voice. Unfortunately, it didn't seem as though she would be finding an ally with her.

"It will only take me a second. I can pee right here." She motioned toward the front of the car. "If you guys just step up there. I'll be two seconds."

Grace frowned.

"Okay," Damon said. "Be quick. I want to get to the hunting shack before it gets dark. I don't want to have to worry about bears."

Yes, the last thing she needed to worry about was another thing that wanted to kill her.

Damon motioned for Grace to move. "Let's give her a second."

"I don't trust her," Grace said, glancing around her and then into the trunk.

Her heart raced with fear that the girl would see her phone and know what she was thinking.

"Come on," Damon said. "And you, April, be my good little girl."

Oh, she was *so* going to make him pay for saying that to her.

As they stepped toward the front of the car, she reached into the trunk and grabbed her phone. She went through the motions of using the restroom. As she squatted, she texted 911.

For the first time since awakening the trunk, she felt hope that she could possibly make it out of this alive.

Chapter Twenty-Four

Sean's foot tapped on the floor of the car as Terrell drove toward the sheriff's department to take his official statement. He didn't want to be here. He didn't want to be playing this game. Yet, he knew Terrell had to check everything off his list.

"Look," Sean said, "all I'm saying is that we run a trace on Damon's phone."

"It's not that simple. The man has burner phones."

He knew it wasn't that simple, but logic wasn't in control. He needed to find April. He had to get her back.

"I know he has her." Sean's foot tapped faster.

"First, there's no proof."

"You know he's been stalking her. She disappeared after a suspicious fire. He was seen leaving the scene of the crime at April's apartment. What other proof do you need?" Sean tried to control his fear-based rage. "You can't possibly think that she started this fire and that she ran away. I thought we've been through that. She is not the one at fault."

Terrell sighed. "I know you are close to her. I know you guys have some kind of relationship happening, but you need to look at this situation from my perspective. I have a job to do, and sometimes that means looking at the story from a variety of perspectives."

"So, you think that Damon was telling you the truth? That he wasn't stalking her? You know he was. You saw the way he looked at her at the Springs. He is a piece of human garbage."

Terrell halted at the stoplight and looked over at him. "I know Damon isn't innocent. I know he was stalking her, but without some kind of witness statement that blatantly states they saw him throwing the Molotov cocktail, I can't get a judge to sign off on a warrant that allows me to go down those rabbit holes. You know this, Sean."

He did. He knew how the justice system worked. But he didn't have to like it.

Terrell's cell phone rang, pulling his attention away from his passenger.

Sean glanced out the window and watched as a mom and daughter walked hand in hand on the sidewalk in front of the small shops that lined the historical downtown.

That could have been April and Grace in another life.

He tried to stop the wave of emotions and thoughts from crashing on him by taking a deep, calming breath.

April couldn't have known that Grace was her daughter. If she had, she would have told him. They'd had so many honest, candid conversations about the past. She'd not hid anything from him that would make him think she'd known that Grace was her daughter. *If* she was her daughter.

Terrell picked up the call. "Hello?"

There was a woman's voice on the other end of the line, and he could tell it was dispatch from the cadence of the words. He tried to listen, but he could only pick up a word here and there.

"Got it. Thanks for the update," Terrell said before hanging up. "Did you hear that?" he asked, turning to face him.

"What's going on?" Sean asked, his core clenching with nerves. Something was wrong. "Is April okay? Did they find her body?"

Terrell shook his head. "Thankfully, no. That's not it at all. Actually, we got a ping from her cell phone. She texted 911."

"What did she say? Is she okay? What happened? Where is she? Damon took her, right?" All of his questions spilled out at once.

"Hold on. All they got was that she needed help." He spoke slowly and carefully, trying to speak in a metered way that Sean knew was to keep him from blowing his top.

"What kind of help? Medical?" he asked, trying to mirror Terrell's tempo to prove that he would be okay, even if everything about the way he was feeling told him otherwise.

"She didn't tell dispatch, just the text and then radio silence. They, however, did manage to pull a location on the device." He flicked on the lights. "We're going to find her."

GRACE WAS STANDING on the side of the trail, looking down at her as she tried to slowly pick her way through the rocks and debris that littered the trail. "You and I both know that you can hike faster than that. I've seen you in action," Grace growled.

Damon put his hand on April's lower back as she stepped beside her. "How's your arm feeling? Are you doing okay?" he asked, sounding like an overly concerned boyfriend and not the man who could just as easily kill her as kiss her.

"I'm okay, just hurting," she said, trying to sound weaker and frailer than she was actually feeling. She ran her arm over her breast, feeling for the phone she'd stuffed in her bra when they hadn't been looking.

"We aren't in a rush, just take your time," he cooed.

Grace rolled her eyes. "She's playing you. She's just fine."

April batted her eyelashes at Damon. "I'll be fine, she's right," she said, stumbling gently and allowing him to help her.

As much as she hated acting like this, especially since she'd been so hell-bent on fighting, she felt as though she was doing the right thing...the thing that this situation required.

"Grace, knock it off," he countered. "She is hurt because of you and your attitude."

Grace's lip curled as she looked down at Damon. "Look, as much as you want to play house, you're not my dad."

April was relieved to see that there was a rift in their alliance. "Wait, playing house?" she asked, her voice soft. "Are you guys—"

"No." Damon shook his head, like any sort of questions about their relationship was out of line and out of the question.

"Why...why all this?" She really didn't understand how the two of them had aligned against her and how she had found herself here if they weren't together in some way.

"Damon, you didn't tell her?" Grace looked at her and smirked, the evil look in her eyes returning. "April, you're my biological mother."

Once again with this girl, it felt as though the ground was giving way under her feet.

Grace couldn't be her daughter. Ann had found a good home, with good parents, people who were going to take care of her and do better than April could have. The adoption agency had told her she was making the right decision, that her daughter would be in good hands.

"What?" April asked, the sound choked and high. "No. My daughter was named Ann. She was adopted by someone out of state. She went to good parents. They promised me…"

"Well," Grace spat, "they lied."

She stared at the girl, trying to find bits of herself or Cameron in her face, but all she could see was a hateful teenager. Maybe, in that, lay the proof that she truly was her child. The only difference was that, at Grace's age, April was pregnant and hoping for a future that had never played out.

"Grace…" She whispered the girl's name like she was speaking it for the first time. "I'm so sorry this happened to you…that I put you in harm's way when I thought I was doing what was best."

Grace waved her off. "You can apologize all you want. It doesn't change a thing." She turned her back on April and started hiking up the hill. "You abandoned me."

This time April didn't hesitate or try to slow their assent. With each step, she moved closer to the girl who claimed to be her daughter.

Damon touched her arm and handed her a tissue. Until now she didn't realize that tears were streaming down her cheeks. "I'm sorry, April. I wanted to tell you before. I thought maybe you knew, but when it was clear you didn't, I knew I had to get you alone with her. I knew we all needed a chance to be a family."

And just like that, regardless of the status of Grace's lineage, she was pulled back to the reality that she and the girl were at the mercy of a man who wasn't in his right mind.

"How did you find out, Damon?" April asked.

"It took some digging after you told me you had given

up a child for adoption. It took a lot of cyber-sleuthing, but I managed to figure out that Grace had been adopted by a family in Cody, Wyoming, a few days after you put up your Ann. A few years later, they moved to Montana for work and when Grace was five, her adoptive parents were killed in a car accident on I-90 and she became a ward of the state of Montana. It was all tough for her after that point. She was moved from home to home."

She made a strangled sound as though his words were a punch straight to her gut. This wasn't what she had wanted for her daughter. And whether or not Grace was Ann, she hated that this had been the girl's past. No child should be treated like chattel and passed around.

"I know that you don't believe me," he continued. "But I ended up running a DNA test on her."

"And me?" she asked, feeling violated as she guessed what he was about to say.

He nodded. "I managed to get a couple hairs of yours. I'm sorry for invading your privacy, but I had to be sure. The results didn't take long, and they were conclusive." He motioned up the hill. "I have all the paperwork in our cabin...even from the state. I'll be happy to show you."

She stared after Grace, watching her move up the hill like she had made this hike many times before. The girl was beautiful, and for the first time she wondered what the girl's natural hair color was—whether it was that of Cameron's or something closer to hers. Her heart ached as she looked at the living reminder of a past she thought was gone forever.

"After I was sure," he continued, seemingly oblivious to the effects his words were having on her heart, "I talked to her foster parents and I made sure that Grace was enrolled at the Springs. I wanted to see you two together. After that, there was no doubt. And I knew what I had to do."

"Damon," she said, knowing she had to be careful in how she approached what she was about to say, "thank you for all of your hard work. You don't know how much I appreciate having the chance to get to know my daughter."

He smiled, his teeth shining brightly in the sun. "I knew you'd appreciate it…that you'd love me for what I'd done."

Love was the wrong word, but she wasn't about to correct him and tell him that what he'd done *terrified* her. Not only was it a complete invasion of both her and Grace's privacy, but he'd upturned two worlds in his unilateral decision to expose the truth. She was truly grateful to finally be reunited with her child, but she hadn't been ready. In finding out this bombshell, it made her feel things that she hadn't been prepared for.

Then again, none of this was really about her.

This was all a game devised by Damon to win her favor.

"How did Grace take the news?" she asked, watching her daughter move behind a ponderosa and disappear into the woods.

"She was upset at first. You know how teenagers can be. She's gone through a lot." He smiled with a weird look of pride—almost like that of a parent. "We spent a lot of time talking about her feelings and what all of this meant to her. She was the one who didn't want to tell you at first. I agreed to give you both time."

"Did she know that you wanted this?" she asked, motioning vaguely at the cabin in the woods.

His features darkened. "Not right away. I had to do a bit of convincing to get her to go along with my idea."

Convincing? Or do you mean grooming? She wanted

to challenge him, but she bit her tongue. She already knew that he'd manipulated the girl and made her an accomplice in his screwed-up game.

"So, she was on board with us being a family?" she asked, playing along.

His smile widened. "She did. This house was her idea. She thought we could use the privacy and get used to being a family. In truth, I think she was really looking forward to it—you know, she'd finally have a bit of stability in her life." He paused, looking up like he was trying to see if she was close and listening. "She was really having a hard time with her foster parents. They were just using her and other kids for a paycheck. They regularly left her, and the other kids who had been in their care, alone."

"Is that why she burned their place down—she was angry?" she asked, though she felt as though she already knew the answer.

"I didn't like the idea, but she was hell-bent." He made a *tsk* sound. "We are going to have to watch her around fire. I think she likes it just a *little bit* too much."

When and if she got them away from Damon, she would make sure Grace got everything she needed—including every therapist and counselor. She thought about several whom she had worked with at the Springs over the years. That was, if Grace safely made it through juvenile court and didn't face charges.

Moving up the mountain, her thoughts were a flurry of what-ifs and hows. She had so many questions, but as her breathing grew labored from the hike, she savored the physical pain as it brought a reprieve from the pain in her soul.

Her well-intentioned past had led to this agonizing present and a potentially even more painful future if Grace hated her or ended up in jail for arson; and her only hope lay in a civil system that had let her down.

Chapter Twenty-Five

Sean had grabbed his pickup and followed behind Terrell up the mountain. It hadn't been hard to find the Toyota Corolla at the bottom of the mountain; it was exactly where 911 had told them it would be after April's text. Unfortunately, as Sean and Terrell walked around the car, it appeared to have been abandoned. There was nothing inside from the visual scan that could give away where Damon had taken her. However, thanks to 911's tracking software, they knew that April's phone was continuing to send a signal, and it appeared as though she was moving up the mountainside.

Their last pin on her phone was about a mile from where he stood and, though he knew they had to be careful in how they approached, Sean wanted to run to her.

When he found her, he wanted to pull her into his arms and beg for her forgiveness. He'd promised he would protect her and keep her from any kind of harm. Instead, he found himself standing beside the car a madman had used to abduct her.

He didn't know what Damon planned to do with her, but if he hurt a single hair on April's head… Damon would pay for what he had done.

Deputy Collins, who had been first on scene, stepped out of his unit. "What are you guys thinking?"

"I think we are going to be in for a hike." Terrell sighed. "It's starting to feel like I'm on patrol again," he added.

Collins gave a dry chuckle. "Don't you miss it? You know, you're always welcome to come back and work the beat with us."

The good-natured ribbing was somewhat of a relief for the tension between the men, but it didn't help when it came to Sean's anxiety. They needed to move. They needed to get to April.

Collins walked up to the trunk of the abandoned blue Corolla and stopped. "Did you see this, Terrell?"

They stepped around, stopping beside Collins. There, barely sticking out of the edge of the closed trunk was the edge of what looked like orange paracord. The end of the cord was frayed and jagged like it had been sawed through. His heart launched into his throat.

"Do you think…" Sean started, trying to control his fear and anger and stop it from smattering his voice. "Do you think Damon had her tied up in the trunk?"

"Let's not jump to any conclusions here." Terrell squatted and stared at the cord for a long moment. "I'm not saying you're not correct in your assumptions, but for now we just need to collect information and get to April."

More than ever before, he feared for April's life. Damon was unstable, and he was capable of just about anything.

Collins took his phone out of his pocket and started taking pictures of the car.

"Are there any other deputies headed this way?" Sean asked.

Terrell nodded. "They are on their way, but as you know it's a bit of a drive."

"Please tell me that we aren't going to wait to go up after

April." He could hear the panic in his tone. "You both have to know that every minute we leave her alone with Damon is a minute closer to her being killed. We have to help her."

That is, if he hadn't killed her already.

She was alive. She had to be alive. As strange as it sounded, he could feel her.

He grabbed his search and rescue pack out of the back seat of his pickup. Say what they will, Andrew hadn't stolen or messed up anything in his rig. The kid would be all right.

From inside his bag, Sean grabbed his holstered Glock 19 and placed it on his belt. He pulled his shirt over to conceal it as much as possible. Closing his pack, he put it on and met up with Terrell and Collins, who were waiting at the start on a barely visible trail.

Terrell was staring at his phone. "It looks like they are moving pretty slow. We should be able to catch up with them in about twenty minutes if we move fast."

"Let's make it fifteen," Sean said, charging up the hill.

The ascent was steep, and the path was nothing more than a game trail. Roots stuck up like grasping hands, threatening to pull him down.

He was breathing hard, and his legs were burning after the first half mile thanks to the pace. He hiked quite a bit with Big Sky Search and Rescue, but short of running he didn't think he could hike any faster. The pain felt good, like it was payment to the Fates to keep the woman in his heart safe until he could reach her.

That was, if her phone was still in her possession.

It was. She was smart.

It struck him, as he led the charge, how this wasn't the first time he had raced up a mountain to get to this woman.

He would do this for her for the rest of his life if it meant she would come home safe—and to him.

She had been through so much. If given a chance, he wanted to be her safe place and the man she could rely on to stand by her side and help her through whatever life threw at them. After their time together, he had to think that she wanted the same.

"Hey, speed goat," Terrell called from behind him, sounding winded, "I know you can run up this hill, but you need to let us be in front in case something happens."

He stopped, waiting for them to catch up. Collins was sweating and laboring for breaths, but he wasn't as bad off as the cherry-faced detective.

Terrell looked at him. "I know you're probably still upset with me, but you don't need to give me a heart attack on this hillside. Damn, man," he said, chuckling.

Sean slapped him on the shoulder. "You know, strangely enough, I am almost enjoying kicking your butt up this hill. Let's call what happened earlier water under the bridge. I know you were just doing your job. I don't have to like it."

"Fair." Terrell gave him an appreciative nod. "You're all right."

"Now, hurry up," he said with a slight grin as he motioned for Terrell and Collins to take the lead. "How far are we out?"

"They haven't moved in a few minutes. I'm thinking they made it to their desired location, or they are taking a break. Either way, we are only about a quarter of a mile to where the phone signal was last picked up." Terrell, in point position, moved up the hill.

Sean's nerves crept up. They were so close.

The men grew silent. The only sounds were of their

feet on the gravel and the rub of their backpacks as they pressed on.

Terrell stopped ahead as they neared the top of the hillside, putting his fist up in the air. He dropped down to his knee and Collins moved into position by his shoulder. Not entirely sure what to do, Sean dropped down to his knee behind the two officers.

As much as he loved to have a little good-natured ribbing with his friends on the police force as to who did the real work, they knew what they were doing—not that he would ever admit that to them.

Terrell whispered something to Collins. They unholstered their weapons, getting into a low-ready position. He looked over his shoulder to him. "You wait here, let us clear the area."

Sean nodded, but he hated that he couldn't be rushing in on the scene with them.

The officers moved to their feet, roll stepping quietly up the trail and moving to the top of the ridge where the mountain saddled out.

"Get down on the ground! Police!" Terrell ordered, using a voice Sean had never heard come out of the cop before.

He moved slowly behind them, staying out of sight, but unholstering his gun in preparation.

Terrell and Collins were pointing their weapons at someone he couldn't see from his position.

"Drop your gun!" Terrell yelled. "If you don't lower your weapon, we will shoot!"

A man released a string of expletives, telling Terrell exactly where he thought they should put their orders and their guns. He recognized the voice as Damon's. "Is Sean with you?" Damon yelled. "If he's with you, I'll trade him for Grace. Then you have to leave."

Grace was with them?

Sean edged upward, unable to control his curiosity but still trying to stay out of the officers' way in case things went sideways. As he moved upward, Damon came into view. He looked crazed, his eyes wide with fear as he stared down the two officers. He had his gun drawn, but it was low by his side.

Grace was standing behind him. Her face was pinched, and there was a smudge of dirt on her cheek. She looked much better than the last time he had seen her, but this time she looked...well, *angry*.

Where's April?

He panicked as he scanned the area. He was tucked behind a small huckleberry bush and some thick bladed grass that obstructed his view. Moving, but careful to stay behind the concealment, he tried to find her.

Where was she? She had to be here. She had to be with Damon.

What if he had killed her and taken her phone?

What in the hell had happened?

His hands started to shake. All he had to do was point and shoot. Damon would be dead.

First, he had to find April. He had to know she was okay. He *had* to.

"Damon, if I come out and trade for Grace, you have to let April go, too!" he said, breaking his concealment.

"Sean?" Damon asked, a dark smile taking over his face.

Damon was going to try to kill him the second he stepped out—that wouldn't help April. He had to be careful.

Collins moved toward him, sticking out his hand like telling him to shut up. Yet, he didn't look away from Damon.

"Is April alive?" Sean asked.

There was a thin line between not putting his brothers in blue in further danger while also making sure that he saved April. As for his life, he would happily exchange his for hers. And he damned well knew that Damon would take the deal, too, as the only thing they had in common was their abnormal love for the same woman.

"If your buddies put their guns down and you show your face, I will let you all see her." Damon put his hand up, almost as though he was telling her to stay put.

"Sean!" April yelled.

She's alive.

He let out a long exhale. That's all he needed to know. Everything else was just details—including Damon's life.

"April, you know better!" Damon countered, looking in the direction she'd called from.

Terrell took that as his moment, and he and Collins charged toward Damon. Sean stood up, weapon ready. As they moved, Grace stepped forward and grabbed at the gun in Damon's hand. He turned to the teenager, a look of surprise on his face. She tried to twist the pistol out of his hand, but he lifted the barrel and pointed it right at the girl's center mass.

"What are you doing?" he stammered, shocked at the girl's sudden change of heart.

"I'm doing what I should have done all along, I'm stopping you. I can't let you destroy anyone else's life." Grace moved closer to the gun.

His finger moved on the trigger.

April came running out and hit Damon square in the back. He made a strangled sound as he lurched forward. Grace grabbed at the gun as he lost his balance, trying to wrestle it out of his hand. As she did, the gun skittered out of Damon's grip and fell to the ground.

Grace lurched for the gun and picked it up. As she moved, the two officers rushed the scene.

They weren't fast enough.

Damon lunged for Grace, murder in his eyes. The girl pointed the gun at him and pulled the trigger.

The sound of the gunfire echoed off the mountain. April looked over at him, fear in her eyes.

Grace stood, motionless. She stared at the man at her feet. "You were never worthy of being a father."

She moved to turn the gun on herself, but Terrell threw his body against hers, throwing her to the ground. Hard.

He pulled the gun out of her hand and threw it to the side and pulled a set of cuffs from his belt. He snapped them on the girl's wrists.

Sean ran to April and pulled her into his arms. She smelled of sweat and fear. He couldn't hold her tightly enough. "You're okay, honey. I've got you. You're safe."

Chapter Twenty-Six

One year later...

The county attorney had decided not to press charges against Grace, calling her actions on the hillside self-defense. In the attorney's statement, they had deemed her roles in the crimes committed by Damon as a product of grooming and manipulation by a man who clearly had mental health problems. As a result for her role in the crimes, they required she seek counseling until she turned eighteen, and moving forward.

Her foster parents, clearly having heard about the fire and Damon's death, hadn't come back. There had been talk that they had cashed out everything they had and fled to Brazil. If they ever returned to the States, or if they were found, charges of negligence and child endangerment awaited them.

Since then, April had been working diligently with members of the state Department of Health and Human Services to create a stronger background check for parents who wished to be licensed foster care providers as well as to help conduct spontaneous inspections for those three thousand kids who were currently in the system in just Montana. It was her goal to make a difference on a national scale in hopes that no child would ever fall through the cracks.

It was her biggest mountain to climb, and she wasn't sure she would ever reach the top or make the kind of difference she wanted, but she wouldn't stop fighting for the kids who felt as though they stood alone. She would forever be their advocate. No kid was perfect, but they all deserved to be treated with decency and given a chance.

For the last year, Cameron's family had refused to have a relationship with Grace and she had been staying with April some nights in her new house and many at the Springs, where she had been working to finish high school. Things between mother and daughter were slowly progressing, but April held out hope that their relationship would keep getting better. No matter what happened legally with her case to adopt Grace, she would be whatever Grace needed her to be—a mom, a friend, a confidant or just a safe place.

Thanks to therapy and time, Grace had granted her forgiveness for the choice she'd made when she was a child—and even younger than Grace was now. April would be forever grateful, and aware that there would still be hard days ahead.

She loved her child just as much as the day she had been placed in her arms.

Today, Grace was staying at her house and lately, things had been going pretty well. Grace was starting to come out of her shell a little more, and today she had even cleaned the kitchen without asking—a major win for any parent, as far as April had been told.

Her house was small, just two bedrooms, but she'd finally managed to get a good deal on her own home and a down payment put together thanks to her renter's insurance payout and savings.

"Grace?" she called.

The girl walked out from the bathroom, drying her naturally blond hair with a towel. "What's up?"

Her daughter had really grown into herself, and she looked more and more like Cameron with each passing day. "Sean and I are going for a hike. He's about to pick me up. Do you need anything while we're out?"

"Give me a second, I'll come with you." Grace moved toward her bedroom. "That okay?" she asked, but not really waiting for an answer.

She loved that her daughter wanted to be a part of her life. It felt like they were becoming a family unit more and more by the day.

"I'll be outside when you're ready," April said, thinking about how lucky she was and how great her life was turning out to be.

Walking outside, she was met with a surprise. Andrew was standing with Sean. They were each holding a hiking pack.

Sean waved at her. "You ready?"

She smiled as she took in his handsome face. "So, Grace told you she wanted to go with us?" She motioned toward Andrew.

Sean's smile widened. "I'm glad she decided to face her fears." He motioned toward the mountain in the distance. "Andrew even picked up everything for a picnic."

The young man lifted the hiking pack in his hand, slightly like it was proof of his kindness.

"Hey, kiddo," she said.

"Hello, Ms. April," he said, lifting the bag and putting it into the bed of Sean's truck.

Sean walked toward her, meeting her halfway from the

front door of her little house, which was starting to become a home. He took her hand and she stepped beside him, expecting him to walk her to his truck. He slipped his hand into hers as she stared up at Lone Mountain, where she had first saved her daughter, and then her daughter had saved her. Those mountains were her home.

"April." He said her name like it was full of unspoken promises.

She could listen to him say her name like that forever.

"Can you believe it was a year ago today?" he asked.

Before she could answer, the door to the house opened and Grace came jogging out. She was pulling her hair behind her head and putting it up with a hair tie. "You didn't do anything without me, did you?"

Andrew groaned. "Seriously? Babe, you're gonna ruin it."

"Not at all," Grace said, laughing as she rushed into the yard. She touched her arm. "Mom, don't listen to him. I'm not going to ruin anything."

April smiled widely, her heart light as Grace called her "Mom." It sounded so beautiful.

Everything about their lives now was a flurry of motion and *life*. It was an ethereal feeling to be in this whirl of activity and love. They were building, all together.

"It's just a hike, guys," April said. "No one's going to ruin it. We're not in a rush." Her thoughts moved to the fateful day on the mountain in the distance that had forever changed all of their lives—in most ways, for the better.

Grace sent her a bright, excited smile and then looked to Sean. "Yeah, just a hike." She giggled.

"What's that supposed to mean?" April asked, looking to Sean.

He had a guilty, excited look on his face.

Andrew jogged over and took hold of Grace's hand. "Babe…"

"Just do it already," Grace urged, looking at Sean.

Sean laughed. "Do you know that your daughter is just a little bit bossy?" he teased, winking playfully at the girl.

Grace stuck out her tongue.

Sean dropped to his knee. "I was going to wait until we were at the top of the mountain, but Grace is right—I can't wait another second."

Her heart thrashed in her chest as she stared down at the most handsome man she had ever laid eyes on. There would only ever be one man who she would see or want.

"April Twofeather," Sean said, "I love you in ways I never knew possible." He pulled a black velvet box out of his pocket. He opened it. Inside was a beautiful channel band fitted with a line of diamonds. It was dazzling, just like him. "You and I have been through hardships in life that most people could never imagine, and yet we have come through it stronger and more in love than any other couple I've ever met. I never want to spend another day without knowing for sure that we will be together forever. Would you marry me? Let's become a family."

She hopped from one foot to the other with pure joy. "Yes, Sean." She looked to Grace and Andrew. "Wait, Grace…"

The teen rolled her eyes. "Come on, Mom, don't you think he already asked me? Of course I told him to do this. I want the best for you. Sean is definitely the best for you. You guys are freaking perfect."

She didn't know if she agreed with the perfect part, but she held no doubts that this moment and this family they had built through hardships and tribulations would be one that stood the test of time.

They were each other's forever.

* * * * *

Look for more books in Danica Winters's Big Sky Search and Rescue miniseries when Winter Warning *goes on sale next month.*

And if you missed the previous titles in the series, you can find Helicopter Rescue *and* Swiftwater Enemies *wherever Harlequin Intrigue books are sold!*